The T

CW00863092

The Talking Head

ELIZABETH PEWSEY

Orion
Children's Books

for Anselm and Eloise

First published in Great Britain in 1996
by Orion Children's Books
a division of the Orion Publishing Group Ltd
Orion House
5 Upper St Martin's Lane
London WC2H 9EA

A catalogue record for this book
is available from the British Library

Typeset in Plantin Light by Deltatype Ltd, Ellesmere Port, Cheshire
Printed in Great Britain by Clays Ltd, St Ives plc

ISBN 1 85881 298 4 (HB)
ISBN 1 85881 299 2 (PB)

One

'WELL, THIS LETTER IS FROM YOUR AUNT Helena.'

Groans.

'She says that she and David are going to Sweden, to a conference.'

'What's new?' said Hal, spreading his hot toast thickly with butter while his mother's attention was on her letter. 'They're always going off to conferences.'

'Hal, not so much butter on your toast.'

How does she know? thought Hal. His mother's eyes didn't work like everyone else's, he had long ago decided. She could even see round corners and up stairs.

'Unfortunately, it isn't one of those conferences where the family can go . . .'

Hal's sister, Gilly, looked up from the cereal packet which she had been reading.

'No,' she said. 'No. Not. Negatives all round. We are absolutely not having horrible Bram here. Not ever again.'

'Gilly, you're making it very difficult for me,' said her mother.

'You promised.'

Her mother sighed. 'I know. I did promise. I promised that I wouldn't invite Bram again. But the case is a bit different.'

'Weasel words, Mum,' said Hal. 'A promise is a promise, and you can't slide out of it by pretending that you only promised not to *invite* him, not to say no when Aunt Helena tried to foist him on us again.'

'I hardly think after last time that he'd want to come again,' said Gilly. 'He must realize how much we dislike him.'

'That's enough,' said their mother, who was beginning to get cross. 'He's your cousin, whether you like it or not. I can understand that you find him difficult to get on with, but that's partly your fault. He can't help being so good at things.'

'Huh!' said Hal. He twitched the letter out of his mother's hand. 'Just exactly what does Aunt H have to say . . .'

His eyes flickered over the neatly-written page. 'The nerve. She isn't even asking if he can come, she's just announcing it. And then all the usual blah, Bram came top in this, that and everything, captain of swimming, captain of cricket . . .'

'Ugh!' said Gilly.

'And what's this? "My niece Erica?" ' Hal gave his mother a dark look as she tweaked her letter out of his hand. 'Who is Erica?'

'Erica is Helena's niece, no relation of yours, although of course she's Bram's cousin, the same as you are.'

'Poor Erica,' said Gilly, but quietly. Mum was very good-natured, but you could push her too far.

Her mother had heard Gilly's remark, but she ignored it. 'Erica is spending the summer with them. She's a bit younger than Bram, about your age, Gilly. Won't that be nice?'

'What has Erica got to do with me?' said Gilly.

—— 2 ——

'Don't be dense,' said Hal, stuffing the last mouthful of toast into his mouth as he pushed his chair back. 'Not only is Bram coming, but this Erica is being dumped on us as well.'

'Yes, she is, and I don't want to hear another word about it,' said their mother. 'You know it upsets your father when you go on about Bram. He doesn't get on very well with Helena himself, but Uncle David is his brother, and he's very fond of him.'

Hal sighed and headed towards the garden door.

'No, Hal. You are not going to spend the morning lolling in the hammock,' said his mother firmly. 'Both of you can go upstairs and tidy up. Bram will have the bed in the loft room as usual, and Erica can go into the spare room once David and Helena have gone – they'll only be here for two nights.'

'And where is this Erica going to sleep for those two nights?' asked Gilly. 'As if I didn't know.'

'She'll sleep on the camp bed in your room. Which means that you will have to clear a space big enough for the bed and for her to get to it.'

'Why can't she sleep on the sofa bed down here?' grumbled Gilly.

'Because she'll be going to bed earlier than we will.'

'Come on, Gilly,' said Hal. 'No point in arguing, you'll worry Mum. How long are they coming for, by the way?'

'Ten days.'

'Ten days of horror,' said Gilly furiously, as they went upstairs.

Hal lounged on the floor of the loft room, undisturbed by the mess around him. 'I'll take that stuff off the bed,' he said, 'and that's it. I shouldn't think Bram will dare to moan about it, not to us, anyway.'

'No, but he'll go on about how untidy we are to his parents and to Mum and Dad,' said Gilly, picking up an armful of books which were strewn across the floor.

The loft room was, in Hal and Gilly's opinion, the best room in the house. It had been converted out of the high-pitched roof of the old, fifteenth-century cottage. They loved the beams and the window at the end that looked out across the countryside, and the spiral staircase which led down to the floor below. Hal kept his model railway there, and the skylight let in just the right light for Gilly's painting. They hated the idea of Bram taking over the loft room even if it was only for ten days.

'Ruining the holidays,' grumbled Hal. 'I had a lot planned, but I shan't do anything if it means Bram is going to drag along.'

Gilly laughed. She knew her brother too well to believe that. 'Lots planned, huh?' she said. 'Like, lying in the hammock, reading, lying up here on wet days, thinking, and sometimes, if you made a great effort, walking as far as the river, for some exhausting fishing.'

'Not true,' said Hal in his lazy way. Little ever ruffled Hal, who was the despair of his teachers and his father. 'He's the most idle boy we've ever had in the school,' his exasperated headmaster had said at the last parents' evening. Gilly, who was as lively as Hal was lazy, couldn't understand his indolent approach to life, but she got very annoyed when other people criticized him.

'Wait and see,' she would say. 'He'll spring into action one day and surprise us all.'

'I hope so,' said their father, with a worried expression on his face. 'I do hope so.'

Looking at her brother now, his lanky frame stretched out on the floor, his eyes closed, Gilly did wonder if anything would ever make Hal spring into action. Well, for a start, she was going to; no way was she clearing up this mess by herself. She placed one foot on Hal's stomach and squeezed him with her bare toes.

'Geroff,' said Hal, without opening his eyes.

'No,' said Gilly. 'Not till you promise you'll wake up and help me get things straight. I know you don't want to, but I'm not doing all this as well as my own room. At least you get to keep your bedroom to yourself.'

'I suppose so,' said Hal, sitting up and pushing Gilly's foot off.

'And if it isn't reasonably clean and tidy, Mum and Dad will get an earful from Aunt Helena, you know how she is about dust.'

'Two days of Aunt H as well as ten days of the other two,' said Hal despondently. He picked up a heap of papers, stacked them together in a rough pile and thrust them into a drawer. 'I don't mind Uncle David on his own, but when they're all together . . . it's grim. Still, maybe this Erica won't be so bad. We shouldn't assume she's going to be awful.'

'Why not?' said Gilly, who had retrieved all the clothes scattered across the floor, and was stuffing them into the linen basket. 'You take this down to the utility, and bring up a wet cloth so I can dust. I don't see how any child of Aunt Helena's sister can be other than ghastly.'

'We'll soon find out,' said Hal with foreboding.

'Bet you ten p I'm right,' said Gilly.

'I owe you ten p,' Hal hissed into Gilly's ear as he passed the potato salad to his aunt.

Aunt Helena and Uncle David had arrived with Bram and Erica quite late in the evening. Supper was salad, so that it didn't matter what time they arrived.

'So right not to bother with a proper meal for us,' murmured Aunt Helena as she looked doubtfully at the potato salad.

Erica's sharp black eyes stared disapprovingly at her aunt's plate. 'You shouldn't eat that,' she said in her clear American voice. 'It doesn't look low-fat to me.'

Uncle David glared at her. He reached out for the potato salad and heaped some on to his own plate.

'And you certainly shouldn't be eating that, Uncle,' said Erica. 'I'm sure you have a cholesterol problem. You're overweight, and your diet is very unwholesome.'

Hal and Gilly stared at her. The nerve, thought Gilly. Fancy telling Uncle David he was overweight. Perhaps he was a bit round, but you could see he didn't like being told he was overweight. She glared at Erica.

'How old are you?'

'Eleven.'

'Well, I think Uncle David, who's at least forty, is old enough to know better than you what he should and shouldn't eat.'

Erica wasn't at all squashed by this. 'As it happens, I'm on an advancement programme back home, so I go to the university every week. One of my subjects there is biochemistry, so I reckon I know a whole lot more about it than Uncle David does. His field is history,' she added with contempt.

'Wow,' said Hal. 'Another genius in the family. Doesn't it make you proud, Aunt Helena?'

Hal's mother shot a warning glance at him before she changed the subject by asking Uncle David about the conference in Sweden.

Gilly looked at the small helping of salad on Erica's plate.

'Is that all you're having? Do you do starvation studies at this university as well?'

'She's a vegetarian,' said Bram, who had been unusually quiet since they had arrived.

'Yes, do you know how unhealthy meat is?' said Erica, looking at the thick slices of ham on Hal's plate.

'Oh, it's not concern for the animals, then?' said Hal.

'Not at all,' said Erica coldly.

'Pity, because we know where this ham comes from, it's a local farmer, and he looks after his animals really well.'

'It makes no difference. I don't eat any animal tissue.'

Hal's mother gave Erica a worried look, and turned to Helena. 'You didn't mention a special diet, I should have got the right food in for her.'

Aunt Helena was even more tight-lipped than usual. 'You'll just have to let her pick and choose, dear,' she said. 'We don't seem to have managed very well, but she has some money. I've told her she may go to the health food shop – I assume you do have one near here? – and buy herself whatever she wants.'

'Oh, that's all right, then,' Mrs Severn said in a weak voice.

Gilly took Erica up to her room. 'You'll only be in here for two nights. When Aunt Helena and Uncle David go, you're to have the spare room.'

'I think they've changed their minds,' said Erica, her eyes fixed on the camp bed. 'I think they plan to leave tomorrow. I can't sleep on that, there's no support for my back. I'll make a bed on the floor.' She sneezed. 'It's very dusty in here, aren't you prone to allergies?'

'No,' said Gilly cheerfully. 'I breathe lots of dust, I eat what I like, and I'm never ill.'

'Wait till you're older,' said Erica. 'You're really building up trouble for your immune system there.'

'I don't know what she's talking about most of the time,' Gilly whispered to Hal as they met outside the bathroom. 'She's so peculiar. She's meditating now.'

'What a freak,' said Hal in disgust. 'Still, there's one good thing, have you noticed that Bram is much better than usual? He hasn't said a word about how brilliant he is at this or that. In fact, he's being almost human.'

'Overshadowed by his weird cousin, I expect,' said Gilly. 'Sssh, here he comes. Do you want the bath-room, Bram? You'll have to wait your turn. Hal was here first, and then it's me.'

A small figure in a cream cotton dressing-gown suddenly swept past them into the bathroom. The bolt shot to with a loud clunk.

'I don't think they know about queuing in America,' said Hal mildly.

'If that's true, then it's the only thing Erica doesn't know,' said Bram gloomily.

'Is she like this all the time?' asked Gilly.

'Oh, yes, she's hardly started. Just you wait. And you've only got to put up with her for ten days. I've got her all summer.'

'She says your parents are only staying for one night,' said Gilly.

'Yes,' said Bram. 'Mother says she'd like to get to

the conference a day earlier, but I know it's really because they can't take any more of Erica.'

'That's mean,' exploded Gilly. 'What about us? I mean, if she's that difficult, how is Mum going to get on with her work?'

Their mother was a translator, and she worked at home.

'Oh, I expect Erica can give her a hand,' said Bram. 'She says she can speak several languages.'

The three of them looked at each other in glum silence.

'We were dreading your coming, Bram,' said Hal frankly, 'but I can tell you that she's far worse than you've ever been.'

Bram flushed. Gilly felt sorry for him; he looked so miserable.

'Yes, I suppose I do go on a bit, but now I see how loathsome Erica is, it makes me want not to be in the least bit like her. And besides, what's the point of Mother telling everyone how brilliantly I did in my exams, and how well I play the piano and so on when Erica's already going to university classes, and she plays concertos and things?'

Gilly giggled. 'At least she can't play cricket.'

'No, that's true,' said Bram brightening. 'Do you know, I scored—'

He stopped abruptly as he saw their faces. 'Sorry. I know you aren't interested. You don't even play cricket, do you, Hal?'

'Oh yes I do,' said Hal. 'Very relaxing game, cricket, as long as the ball doesn't come anywhere near you.'

'I vote we try to keep her in her place while she's here,' said Gilly.

'Sssh!' said Hal warningly. 'She's coming.'

Erica came out, leaving a strange, seaweedy smell drifting behind her.

'What's that?' said Hal, wrinkling his nose.

'Oh, it's some guk she uses instead of soap. Don't mention it, or she'll go on at you for hours about how the skin works, and cell renewal.' Bram moved forward towards the bathroom door. 'Am I next?'

'No,' said Gilly as the door shut behind him.

'Never mind,' said Hal. 'Perhaps that peculiar smell will have faded by the time he's brushed his teeth.'

'Bet Erica uses liquorice toothpaste,' said Gilly sleepily.

'Is there such a thing?' said Hal.

'Yes, I've seen it in the shops. Sugar-free, no chemicals . . . you know.' She yawned. 'I hope Bram hurries up. I need a good night's sleep, I can see we're going to need all our energy.'

'You can go in next,' said Hal generously. 'I'm planning to sleep in tomorrow.'

Two

*H*AL WASN'T GIVEN THE CHANCE. UNCLE DAVID and Aunt Helena were leaving that day, but not until the evening. Uncle David wanted to visit an exhibition which was being held at the castle, and he thought they could all go.

'I'll stand you lunch,' he said.

'Won't cost you a lot for Erica's share,' said Mr Severn. 'Not judging by last night. But I think we'd all enjoy the castle, David. We haven't been for a couple of years, and I hear this exhibition is very interesting. Are they awake yet, Fran?'

She shook her head. 'Hal won't wake up for hours yet. I don't know about the others. I think I heard someone playing the piano . . .'

'Erica, I expect,' said Uncle David with a sigh. 'She doesn't seem to need much sleep. She tells us it's because she's so intelligent.'

Hal's parents exchanged speaking looks. 'I'll go and get Hal up,' said Mr Severn. 'We haven't got a lot of time if David and Helena have to get to the airport this evening.'

'Take a wet sponge,' advised Hal's loving mother. 'Be firm. And David, it's kind of you to offer, but it's such a lovely day, let's have a picnic. You can buy ice-creams and something to drink.'

'It's a deal,' said Uncle David cheerfully. 'I'll see if I can find a herbal concoction for Erica.'

'Hemlock juice,' suggested Mr Severn as he set off upstairs.

'Castle?' said Erica sharply, when she learnt about the plans for the day. 'I'm not interested in castles. I did medieval warfare at school. Our teacher said you British spend too much time worshipping the past.'

'I think he was right,' said Aunt Helena, who had a very modern outlook.

'Too bad,' said Uncle David, quite crossly for him. 'This castle is well worth seeing. It's thirteenth century, built on the site of an earlier Celtic fortress. That's why they're having this exhibition. They've just finished a very successful excavation there. Anyway, we're all going, so I don't want to hear any more complaints.'

'You'll enjoy the walk,' Aunt Helena told Erica.

It was a stiff climb up the hill to the castle. There was a car park at the bottom, but they had come across the fields, Hal and Bram taking turns to carry the coolbox.

'Good thing I'm fit,' said Bram, who was more his old self this morning.

Hal looked at him with scorn. 'You may be fit, but you're hotter than I am, and you're puffing more than I am,' he said. 'All this running about on the games field doesn't really do you any good.'

Erica, who was moving effortlessly up the hill, stopped to look round at the two boys. 'Exercise is essential for your heart function,' she told Hal. 'If you don't do regular physical activity, you should at least get to work out at the gym three or four times a week. I do regular aerobic training and work-outs, I'm in the State Junior Team for swimming, and I hold several junior records in athletics.'

Gilly was walking alongside her mother. She made a face at her, to show what she thought of what Erica had said, but her mother, who was deep in conversation with Uncle David, took no notice. Aunt Helena, who was another know-all, was walking alongside Gilly's father and telling him a lot of things he wasn't the least interested in.

Pity she ever married Uncle David, Gilly said to herself. If he'd married someone else, we wouldn't have to put up with Erica and Bram.

'You may be a wonder athlete,' she said rudely to Erica, 'but I can tell you that you look very odd, with that white paste all over you.'

Erica was indeed a startling sight. She was wearing a long-sleeved shirt and cotton trousers, and had put white cream over any patch of skin that showed. So she had white ankles and hands, and under her floppy hat all you could see of her nose was a white triangle of cream.

Erica wasn't bothered. 'The sun's rays are very harmful,' she said, looking disapprovingly at Gilly's brown legs. 'You're just asking for trouble, Gilly, wearing shorts with no sun cream on. You should be wearing a sun block, like I do, or at least a cream with a protection factor of twenty or so.'

'I never burn,' said Gilly. 'So there isn't a problem.'

'You'll regret it when you're older,' said Erica. 'I plan to have a youthful skin even when I'm forty.'

'No need to worry about that,' Hal whispered to Bram. 'Someone will have murdered her long before she gets to forty.'

At the entrance to the exhibition, Mrs Severn hesitated. 'I think it would be better if we didn't all go round together,' she said. 'Why don't you young ones go round on your own? Then we can meet up back here – say in an hour?'

'I may need more than an hour,' said Uncle David as he pulled out his wallet to pay for the tickets. He waved Mr Severn away. 'No, no, my treat. Four adults and four under-fourteens, please,' he said to the woman at the ticket desk. 'And two guidebooks.'

He gave one of the guidebooks to Hal. 'There you are, you take them round, although I expect Erica will know all about the Celts.'

Erica turned a cold eye on her uncle. 'I did a project on The Celts, Fact and Fiction,' she said. 'It won a prize.'

'There you are, then. You can tell the others all the Celtic myths,' said Uncle David genially. 'They're fascinating.'

'Facts are fine,' said Erica. 'Myth is a reversion to a childish and out-dated need for supernatural beliefs. I have no time for myth.'

'Oh, good, that's quite clear then,' said Hal, laughing as Uncle David winked at him.

'You go that way,' said his father. 'And we'll go in this direction. See you in an hour.'

Gilly trailed along behind the other three. Erica was sounding off about Celtic cults. Bram was trying to make knowledgeable and intelligent comments, which Erica ignored. Hal ambled along in his usual unruffled way, although Gilly did notice his mouth twitch once or twice.

They came to an exhibit of a carved head which was displayed on top of a column at eye level.

'The severed head played an important part in Celtic culture, ritual and belief,' began Erica.

'Oh, shut up,' muttered Hal. Gilly saw him give a quick beckoning gesture with his hand, and she joined him as they stealthily moved away.

'Phew,' he said, as they rounded the corner. 'Let's leave them to it.'

They wandered on, pleased to be away from the other two. 'This is quite interesting,' said Hal presently. 'At least, it is when you haven't got someone yakking in your ear about it.'

'I read some Celtic legends once,' said Gilly dreamily. 'They were fantastic. People riding into a mist and finding themselves in another world. Poor old Erica, if she can't enjoy things like that.'

'Don't suppose she enjoys anything much,' said Hal. 'The world's full of danger – food, the sun, myths . . .'

They were going past a narrow entrance with a door.

'Let's go in here,' said Gilly.

'I don't think that's part of the exhibition,' said Hal. 'It's probably the broom cupboard or something.'

Gilly gave the door a push. 'No, it's OK, it's open, and look, it *is* part of the exhibition.'

'Only one exhibit, though,' said Hal.

The three big stones stood alone in the centre of the room. With two shorter upright stones, and a great slab set across the top, they formed a rough arch. It was dramatically lit from the walls and ceiling with spotlights.

Hal read the information printed on the placard which stood beside the stones.

'*Entrance to an ancient Celtic burial chamber,*' he read aloud. '*This portal tomb is typical of a type found in several parts of Ireland.*'

'No actual burial chamber, though,' said Gilly, craning her neck to look through the stones. 'No bodies.' She stepped back to join Hal, who was leaning against the wall, looking thoughtfully at the stones.

'There's something about them, isn't there?' he said at last.

'Yes,' said Gilly. 'They're eerie, somehow.' She shivered. 'It's very cold in here, I'm sure it wasn't as cold as this in the other rooms.'

'Maybe the thermostat's gone wrong,' said Hal practically. 'These museums have very complicated electronic controls. Everything has to be kept at the right temperature and humidity, so as not to damage any of the pieces.' He paused. 'I think there is something wrong, though. The air smells funny.'

'It does,' agreed Gilly. 'And look, it's misty! How can it be misty? Is it smoke?'

'Doesn't smell like smoke,' said Hal. 'Very strange. Perhaps we'd better go and see if we can find someone.'

They went towards the door; then Gilly stopped abruptly. 'Bother,' she said. 'I can hear voices. I think it's Bram and Erica. Let's wait and hope they go past.'

The voices came nearer, and the footsteps stopped outside the door.

'Quick,' said Gilly. 'Let's hide behind the stones. They may miss us. It's so cold in here I don't expect even Erica will want to stand and jabber on about it.'

'They couldn't see anything anyway,' said Hal. 'Not with this mist floating around. And the notice does say, "*Please do not touch*".'

'Who's touching?' said Gilly. 'We're just going to hide until the enemy has gone past.'

She stepped across the low rope in front of the stones and went through the archway. Hal, with a quick backward look, followed her just as the dim shapes of Bram and Erica appeared in the doorway to the room.

'Look,' said Gilly, her voice high and surprised.

Hal put a finger on his lips and frowned. 'They'll hear you.'

'Look!' said Gilly again, pulling Hal round.

Hal blinked with disbelief. He shut his eyes, shook his head and looked again.

'Brilliant,' he said. 'It's brilliant. How did they do this?'

Instead of the rough stone wall of the castle facing them, they were outside. It was hotter than ever and there was a haze of heat across the landscape.

'Amazing,' said Gilly. 'It's a way out. I hope they'll let us back in again. I haven't got enough money to buy another ticket.'

'Gilly,' said Hal. 'Where's the car park?'

Gilly looked down the hill. 'It must be on the other side. You can't see it from here.'

'And where's the castle?'

Gilly looked at Hal in astonishment, and then she saw what he meant. She had been so busy sniffing the warm air and looking out across the countryside that she hadn't noticed that the only building of any kind to be seen was the stone archway. No soaring thirteenth-century walls, no towers, no ramparts. Nothing at all, except the three great slabs of stone which they had just come through.

Gilly hesitated for a moment, and then, taking a

deep breath, she walked towards the arch. She bent down and looked through it.

'Hal,' she said. 'It's all changed. The castle room isn't there. This leads into a kind of chamber. It's like the photo of the inside of the burial chamber which we were looking at in the exhibition.'

Hal bent down to look as well. He stood up, and dusted his knees. Then he saw Gilly staring over his shoulder. She had a look of astonishment on her face, and he slowly turned round, wondering what on earth she could have seen.

Three

*I*T WAS A BOY, ABOUT HAL´S AGE, WHO WAS standing looking at them with grave, dark eyes.

'What enemy?' he said.

'Enemy?'

'You said, "We're just going to hide until the enemy has gone past." '

'Yes,' said Gilly. 'I said that. It wasn't an enemy, really. Just our cousin, and his cousin.'

The dark boy looked puzzled. 'Cousins? How can cousins be enemies? And isn't your cousin's cousin your cousin?'

'Not exactly,' said Hal. 'You see,' he went on, and then he stopped. 'It doesn't matter. Who are you? Are you still at the castle? What's going on? Is it some kind of historical event. Are you acting scenes from the past?'

The boy laughed. 'No,' he said. 'I'm not an actor. And I'm not from the past, either. I'm now, the same as you, but I think it's a different now from your now.'

Gilly had been looking over the whole sweep of the countryside, with a thoughtful expression on her face. 'Hal, this is different. At first it seems the same, but when you look at it again, really look, it isn't. The light is different. The colours are different.'

'Nonsense,' said Hal. 'How can it be different?'

'It's different because it is different,' said the boy.

'Are you saying this is another world? Are you saying we've died?'

'No, no. It isn't *another* world, just a different one. One that you don't normally see. There are places where the mist comes, and then . . . Well, you slip through.'

'There was a mist,' said Gilly. 'In the room in the castle.'

'Yes, there's always a mist when people slip through. We keep away from the mists, you never know where you might end up. Did you come through the burial chamber?'

'I think so,' said Gilly. 'Only there were just the three stones, in an arch. We were in the museum, at the castle. There was no chamber, it wasn't as it is now.'

'So. There was a mist, and you walked through the archway of three stones? It's not surprising that you're here. Don't you know not to walk into the mist? Don't your people teach you about these things?'

'I can't say it's a subject that's ever come up,' said Hal. He laughed, imagining a school where instead of PSD lessons they learned about the dangers of mist and the properties of stone archways.

'What's PSD?' asked the boy.

'Personal and Social Development,' said Hal. 'Awful rubbish.' He looked thoughtfully at the boy. 'Actually, I didn't say anything about PSD.'

'No, but you thought it.'

'Can you read minds?' said Gilly, curiously.

'Sometimes,' he said.

'What's your name?' said Gilly. 'And why are you looking depressed?'

'I'm Lugh. I'm not depressed, just worried.'

'I'm Gilly. This is Hal. He's my brother. So, what's the matter?'

'There's a problem, that's all. It needs something done about it, which I can't do.'

'Can we help?' asked Gilly.

Hal sighed. 'Gilly, all we can do is sit here, or better still, lie here, peacefully, and wait until the castle reappears and we can go back to normal.'

'That won't be possible,' said Lugh. 'The mist has gone. So has the archway, at least in the form which you came through. No, I'm afraid you can sit and lie as long as you like. All that will happen is that you'll get very hot and hungry.'

'Oh,' said Hal. It didn't sound like his idea of a good day.

'Or you can come with me, to my village, which isn't far away.'

Without really intending to, they found themselves following Lugh as he set off down a steep path which led down the hill.

He wasn't going to admit it, but Hal had the feeling that Gilly was right. It was different. Not strange or exotic, but the shape of things was different, the way the path went, and many of the flowers and trees were unfamiliar. Then there was the heat. It wasn't an English heat, it was more like the Mediterranean. He caught up with Lugh.

'If this is now, if we're in, what do they call it . . . a parallel universe, then what about time?'

'I don't know about parallel universes,' said Lugh. 'Mostly, we find it's best just to concentrate on our world, and let the universe look after itself. I don't know what universe I'm in, or whether it's the same as yours, or parallel. Best not to enquire, I'd say.

—— 21 ——

Time . . . Ah, you're worried that when, or if, you get back to your own place—'

'When, not if.'

'—will the same time have passed there as here? You have family who'll be worried about you if you're gone for a long time. They'll be out looking for you, setting up a hue and cry over the countryside?'

'Something like that.'

'Who can say? Mostly, time here is different. Since you're spending time here, and not there, you haven't lived this time where you come from, and so no time has passed. That's usually the way it works.'

'Does this happen often, then? People slipping through?' asked Gilly. She wished she had her paint box with her. The light and shapes and shadows were fascinating, and she longed to paint them.

'You couldn't stop and paint now, even if you had your painting equipment, could you?' said Lugh practically. 'And I doubt if you've slipped through just to paint, although of course with artists you can never tell. Yes, people do slip through. More from you to us than the other way round. You don't know how to call us, mostly, you see. And we find it a bit cold and damp where you come from. The climate doesn't suit us.'

'Called?' said Hal. 'Were we called?'

'Oh, yes.'

'I thought it was the mist and the arch,' said Gilly. 'Some sort of magic.'

'Magic? It is magic, in a way, but not ordinary magic. You have to be called. Perhaps I called you, without realizing it.'

'Don't you know?' said Hal. 'Whether you called us or not?'

'Do you always know what you want? Surely not. Besides, now I come to think about it, I did call for help

— 22 —

a little while ago. I'm not sure that you were the kind of help I had in mind, but then they like a joke.'

'Who likes a joke?'

'Everyone likes a joke. Don't you like a joke?'

Gilly shook her head. She didn't think that Lugh's mind worked in the same way as hers and Hal's. 'What's the problem?' she said. 'Maybe we can help, after all.'

Lugh looked doubtful. 'I'll show you by and by. First, I'll take you to my village. Then we'll go and see if he's still there.'

'Who's still there?'

'You'll see,' said Lugh infuriatingly. 'We cross the river here, at the ford. There is a bridge, but it's a long way round, and the river isn't high at the moment.'

Gilly and Hal stopped at the edge of the shallow water of the ford to take off their shoes. Lugh looked with interest at Hal's trainers. 'You have very big feet,' he said. 'Big hands, too.'

'So?' said Hal. He didn't like people commenting on his hands and, especially, his feet.

'So, you have big hands and feet. A fact. Nothing to worry about. Those shoes must be hot. I'll see if I can find a pair of sandals in the village for you.'

'I won't wear sandals,' said Hal, enjoying the cool water running over his feet.

'Then your feet will be hot and you'll get blisters.'

Gilly laughed. 'Not Hal,' she said. 'Hal never walks far enough to get blisters.'

'No?' said Lugh. He watched while Hal dried his feet as much as he could on the grass before putting his trainers back on. Lugh's own clothes were unusual to Hal's and Gilly's eyes; a loose tunic over what looked like a long pair of shorts. He wore rather Roman-looking sandals; Gilly thought Hal was mad to refuse to wear sandals if Lugh meant a pair like that.

There was a building just beyond the ford, a substantial building which could have been a farm. It looked well-kept, but was obviously unoccupied, with shutters closed on the windows, and no signs of life. Gilly noticed the anvil standing beneath an open barn which ran along beside the house.

'It's a smithy,' she said. 'Where's the smith?'

'Gone, like all the rest,' said Lugh sadly.

'All the rest? Who? What do you mean?' said Hal.

'You ask a lot of questions,' said Lugh. 'You'll see.'

The village was about half a mile further down the road. It had a prosperous look to it, and wasn't at all the kind of village of primitive huts and muddy roads that Hal had been imagining. The houses were stone-built, and painted in light colours. To keep the heat out, thought Gilly. I bet it gets really hot here. It reminds me of a Mediterranean village, like the one we stayed in last year in Spain.

'You see, we aren't living in the past here,' Lugh said. 'We aren't primitive.'

'No, we can see that,' said Gilly quickly. 'Why is it so quiet? Does everyone have a siesta here, like in Spain?'

Lugh shook his head. 'No, there's no one here to have a siesta,' he said. 'There's only me and my aunt left. She's a witch, so she thought she didn't need to go.'

'Witch?' said Gilly, in tones of disbelief.

'Yes, witch. Me,' said a grating voice behind them. Gilly and Hal whirled round, coming face to face with a large old woman, all too like a story-book witch with a big, jutting nose and chin.

'I don't believe in witches,' said Gilly defiantly, and a minute later, Hal was hopping round her feet in the shape of a large toad.

'Hal,' she shrieked. 'Hal!'

'Oh, stop it, Mab,' said Lugh in a weary tone of voice.

'Is this what they sent to help you?' said the witch, snapping her fingers and making Hal reappear in his normal shape.

Gilly clutched him. 'Oh, Hal, are you all right?'

'Of course I'm all right. What are you going on about?'

'She turned you into a toad.'

'Toad? Don't be silly.'

Lugh came to their rescue. 'She made you think Hal was a toad, just a trick.'

The witch sniffed. 'Trick? You be careful, young Lugh.'

'Why did she turn Hal into a toad when it was me who said I didn't believe in her?'

'Because she didn't turn anyone into a toad, she just made you think he was a toad. What would be the point of making Hal think you were a toad; that wouldn't be getting her own back on you, would it?'

'I don't understand,' said Gilly.

'Come on, Mab,' said Lugh crossly. 'Stop playing games.'

'All right,' said the witch, and changed herself into a normal, middle-aged woman.

'What is going on?' said Hal.

'When I said she was a witch, you saw her as you think witches are meant to be. Likewise, witches where you come from turn people into toads, so she obliged.'

'Only she didn't really do anything,' said Hal, slowly.

'No,' said Lugh.

'But there aren't witches where we come from,' cried Gilly.

'How do you know?' said the witch. 'If you saw me at the supermarket on a Saturday morning, you wouldn't say to yourself, "Ha, a witch," would you?'

Gilly, who had been thinking that the witch was now the image of her maths teacher, looked alarmed.

'Don't worry, dear,' said the witch. 'We in the sisterhood never bother you if you don't bother us.'

At that she disappeared.

'Where's she gone?' said Hal, relieved.

'I don't know,' said Lugh. 'Off to do some mischief, I expect.'

He sounded rather despondent, Gilly thought. Perhaps it wasn't easy having a witch for an aunt.

They had been walking slowly on, and had come to a wide square with a fountain in the centre. Like the rest of the village, the square was deserted. Hal headed for a stone bench and sat down.

'No further,' he said firmly, 'till you tell us what's going on.'

Gilly joined him on the bench. 'Can we drink the water?'

Lugh looked suprised. 'Of course. Why not?' There were some pottery beakers on the little wall which surrounded the fountain. Lugh held two under the cascading water, and then handed them to Gilly and Hal. 'Are you hungry, as well?'

'No,' said Gilly. 'What we really want is to know what's going on.'

Four

LUGH LEANT AGAINST ONE OF THE SLENDER trees growing along the edge of a sandy path which went round the fountain.

'As you can see, there's no one here. Everyone's gone.'

'Except you,' said Hal.

'And your aunt,' said Gilly.

'Yes,' said Lugh, without enthusiasm.

'So where have they gone, and why?'

Lugh moved over to a second bench which was at right angles to the one they were sitting on. He sat sideways, clasping his knees with his hands.

He looks uneasy and uncertain, thought Gilly. Something's really getting to him.

'I don't know where to begin,' said Lugh. 'You see, you don't know anything about our history, and this goes back a long way.'

Gilly sensed a story and wriggled herself into a more comfortable position. Gilly liked a good story.

'There are two nations who live in this country, the Tuans – that's us – and the Vemorians,' said Lugh. 'We're quite similar in some ways; we look the same, and speak the same language more or less, but we're still different in all kinds of ways. The Tuans and the Vemorians have never really got on. In the past, they used to fight a lot: border raids, disputed lands, piracy at sea, that kind of thing. The Vemorians are organized, cold and hard, and we Tuans aren't, so they always thought it would be good for us if they took us over and ran Tuan properly.

'Colonialists,' said Hal knowledgeably.

'We Tuans enjoy life, and as far as we're concerned, the Vemorians don't, and we aren't about to change our ways. Anyway, it hasn't worried anybody for ages, because a long time ago, the Tuans and the Vemorians made a truce. They agreed: no more border raids, no more kidnapping people and making them into slaves—'

Gilly was horrified. 'Slaves? Lugh, you don't have slaves.'

'No, but the Vemorians do. Much cheaper owning people than having to pay them. They used to nab people who lived near the border, and spirit them away. A long time ago, as I said. Let me finish. We'd leave their ships alone, they'd stop trying to take us over for our own good, and we Tuans wouldn't practise any magic on them.'

'Magic, again,' said Hal with a sigh.

'This truce was witnessed by the gods when it was made, and so it was inviolable.'

'What does that mean?' asked Gilly.

'It means it couldn't be broken under any circumstances,' said Hal. 'Go on.'

'It's worked for as long as anyone can remember. The Vemorians still think Tuan would be better off if they were in charge, we think the Vemorians are cold fish who have no fun and don't understand magic, but the truce has held. People could travel from one country to the other, they bought things from us and vice versa.'

'And?' said Gilly, impatiently.

'Not long ago, Vemoria began to ignore the truce. Just in a small way to begin with, moving a boundary here, taking over a village or a hill there. By the time we Tuans realized what the Vemorians were up to, we'd lost a lot of land.'

Lugh swung down from his bench, and picked up a twig. Gilly and Hal watched, intrigued, as he drew the outline of a map in the fine sand on the ground around the fountain.

'This is Tuan, it's a kind of C shape, encircling Vemoria. Vemoria is here. These were the ancient boundaries. You can see that Tuan is almost divided in two, but there hasn't been any trouble for years about getting from one side to the other because of this strip of land.'

Hal and Gilly could see what he meant. 'What's on the other side of that narrow bit of land?' asked Hal. 'Sea?'

'No,' said Lugh. 'This is the coast, here. That part of Tuan joins the Third Lands.'

'Who lives there?'

Lugh thought before answering. 'The gods,' he said finally.

Hal and Gilly stared at him, disbelief written all over their faces.

Lugh pulled a face. 'I'll explain about them in a minute,' he said, returning to his sand map.

'The Vemorians aren't stupid. Once they'd taken some land and a few villages, and nothing happened, they attacked here – ' and Lugh pointed to the narrow piece of land – 'and separated the two halves of Tuan.'

'Awkward,' said Hal, bending down beside Lugh. They looked at the outlines in the sand. 'You could get between the parts of Tuan by sea, couldn't you?' said Hal.

Lugh shook his head. 'No, the Vemorians have been building ships in a big way. They've now got a very powerful fleet, and they set up a blockade before they moved in to chop us in half.'

'Where's your village?' asked Gilly.

'Here. Right on the edge of Vemoria, now, although of course it never used to be a border village.'

'Can't you fight back?' asked Hal. 'Fend them off?'

'Our strength doesn't lie with weapons and armies,' said Lugh. 'The reason the truce has held, and the reason we've always been safe, is that we have a special power. It's a kind of magic, but not what *you* think of as magic. We can control all kinds of forces, or at least, we used to be able to control them. Like I said, the Vemorians are very efficient, and ruthless, and good at organizing, and wonderful at anything to do with water. You should see their canals. But they have absolutely no magic powers. Not the kind we have. They used to have some, people say, but that was before their present rulers took power. They've always been very afraid of magic. It isn't logical, you see.'

'No, I don't see,' Hal said under his breath.

Lugh looked at him. 'No, perhaps you don't,' he said with a sigh. 'You don't have any magic left where you come from, so it's difficult to understand. Just keep an open mind, that's all.'

'Not so easy,' said Gilly. 'So, if this magic is what keeps the Vemorians off your backs, why are they able to attack you and take your land?'

'It's all changed,' said Lugh. 'Our powers have been seeping away, nobody's quite sure how or why. The only ones who still have real magical powers are the witches, and you can see how useless they are; a bunch of dotty types, that's all. It isn't the kind of magic that would help to fend off the Vemorians.'

Gilly didn't know what to say. How could they believe all this talk of magic? It was absurd! On the other hand, she and Hal had been transported here, in a twinkling of an eye . . .

'Yes, I can see it's strange for you,' Lugh went on. 'It always is for people who come through from your world. The magic, I mean. I can't prove it to you, not the way things are. I'm supposed to be a soothsayer, and I was pretty good when I was younger. Now I can hardly do anything. The future's a blur, and I mostly haven't a clue what other people are doing. It's hopeless.'

'Oh dear,' said Gilly. 'So the Vemorians will just walk in and take over?'

'Yes,' said Lugh miserably. 'If they go on like this, they'll reach here' – and he pointed to a place in the other part of Tuan – 'and take the Walled City. That's like your capital, I suppose, only it's more than that. It's very old, and sacred. I would have gone there, for training, when I was fourteen.'

'You said the truce had been made by the gods. What's happened to them?'

'Who can say? Besides, the Vemorians are being very stealthy about it. Some people say that some of the immortals are siding with the Vemorians. Wouldn't be the first time, they're a tricky lot. If the Vemorians are trying to hide what they're up to, then, frankly, it's a waste of time. The gods are very curious and gossipy, and some of them must have noticed something. Unless they're just too busy arguing among themselves at the moment to bother with us.'

'Who are these gods?' said Gilly, fascinated.

'They're the Third Race. They live on the other side of these mountains, here. They're supposed to keep an eye on things, but they lead very quarrelsome lives themselves. By and large, it's live and let live; we don't cross them, and they don't bother us. Then they get het up about something and start to interfere in the affairs of us mortals. Bad news, because they nearly always make matters much worse.'

'Oh,' said Gilly, who had quite a different picture in her mind of what mythical gods would be like. 'Can they do whatever they like? Do they control this strong magic you told us about?'

'Nobody controls the strong magic. Ultimately, they're bound by it, the same as us. But they do have all kinds of powers that we don't. Of course they do,' he added almost irritably. 'They're immortal or semi-immortal, for a start. That makes a difference. Then they're bigger and stronger than we are. Some of them are very intelligent, although there are some real clunks among them, too.' Lugh shook himself. 'I'd rather not think about them, and we mostly don't. Then something like this happens, and you have no choice.'

'It's all very complicated,' complained Hal. 'Have the Vemorians taken over your village? Is that what's happened? Where are they? Where are the villagers? Why are you still here?'

'When the Vemorians target a village, they start by kidnapping key people. All the useful people get taken. Then, when things in the village start to break down, they move in.'

'What happens to the people they kidnap?' asked Gilly. 'And the villagers, when the Vemorians take over?' She didn't much like the sound of this.

'They're enslaved.'

'Have they taken any of your family?'

'A few. Some cousins.'

'Lucky you,' said Gilly, thinking of Bram and Erica.

'I'm not from this village, though,' Lugh went on. 'I came here to be brought up by my mother's brother. That's what usually happens.'

'Are your parents all right? Have you got any brothers or sisters?'

'Oh, really, Gilly,' burst out Hal. 'What does it matter?'

'I have, yes,' said Lugh. 'As far as I know, they are still all right; the Vemorians haven't reached there yet.' He paused, and then went on, looking across the square as he spoke. 'They started the kidnappings here a little while ago. Then the villagers decided to fight, rather than just be taken into slavery.'

'Good for you,' said Hal.

'Pointless, I should think,' said Gilly.

'Gilly's right, in one way, but not in another,' said Lugh. 'You see, two nights ago, on the evening before the battle, something very strange happened.'

'What?' said Hal impatiently, as Lugh fell silent.

Gilly could see the heart of the story coming, and she slid to the ground, scuffing the map.

'We'd all been running around like ants,' said Lugh, 'because we knew the Vemorians had targeted our village. We were trying to sort out some weapons and find what we could to use as armour. We Tuans don't do much military training, not like the Vemorians. For them, it's drill, drill, drill from the time they're about seven years old. We never thought we'd need to fight, you see, so we only had a vague idea of what to do.'

'Unwise,' said Hal, rolling on his back. He always listened better like that.

Lugh went on with his story. 'The villagers had

— 33 —

decided to have a feast in the great hall. That's that building over there.'

Hal and Gilly looked across to where Lugh was pointing.

'A last banquet before the battle?' said Gilly approvingly. She was always one for the dramatic gesture.

'Amazing doors,' said Hal, looking over to the hall. 'Is it big inside?'

Lugh nodded, and went on. 'We were past being frightened by then and we were all in a good mood. Tuans always cheer themselves up with music and story-telling; we like having a good time. It was getting noisy, and so no one heard the knocking at the door to start with. Then it got louder, and my uncle told me to go and see who was making such a racket.

'Before I got to the doors, they suddenly flew open, giving everyone a bit of a shock. There was a man, huge, just standing there between the doors. The hall went absolutely silent, everyone was so amazed. It was a stranger, but he was enormous, far bigger than any human. For a moment, everyone thought the Vemorians had come, but this man was no Vemorian. He was too big, and far too beautiful. He had wild red hair and strange green eyes.

'His eyes swept over us all, and he walked slowly up to the top table. His voice wasn't loud, but we could all hear every word.

"I have come to fight for you," he said. "I will lead you tomorrow, and with my help, you will drive the Vemorians away. However, there is one condition: if I should be killed, you must cut off my head."

'That proposal didn't go down at all well, because it's considered very bad luck to be buried without your head. Bodies that are buried in two pieces don't stay

quietly in the grave, they come back to haunt respectable friends and relatives. They didn't fancy having
this huge man's ghost flitting around in bits.

'Still, they said to each other, who would be able to
kill someone that size? By the look of him, he was an
immortal, and in that case, there would be no question
of anyone having to cut off his head.

'It was a deal.'

Hal propped himself up. 'Sounds like a good one to
me. What happened then?'

'The huge man left, promising to be there the next
morning, and we all went off to bed, feeling quite
cheerful about the next day.'

'Did he come back?' cried Gilly, enthralled. 'Did he
fight for you?'

'Oh, yes, he came back all right,' said Lugh. 'I wasn't
allowed to fight; soothsayers aren't, even if they aren't
doing much in the way of soothsaying. I watched,
though. The Vemorians came surging over the hill, all
in immaculate rows, the way they do . . . They didn't
have a hope, he just tossed them about, no trouble at
all. It wasn't long before they all went shrieking and
yelling away, taking their dead and injured with them.

'We had lost a few men, very few, considering. The
huge man had disappeared, which was very convenient. Then, as we were bringing people down to the
village, we found his body, just lying there.'

'How had he been killed?' asked Hal. 'If he was so
strong?'

'I'm not sure,' said Lugh. 'He must have fallen in
battle, although he didn't seem to have any injuries.
Nobody wanted to investigate too closely.'

'So you cut off his head?' said Gilly.

'Now that's the problem,' said Lugh. 'Once the
threat from the Vemorians was over, people began to

have second thoughts. They worried about what he might do in the haunting line. They talked it over – we're great talkers. Then they started arguing. My uncle thought we had to keep our word, but most of the other villagers, and the village priest, who's very stupid and obstinate, said, no, he had saved us, we had to give him a proper burial, with head attached.

'While they were still discussing it, my aunt appeared. With bad news. She'd been having a quiet flit round, seeing how things stood. And although the Vemorians had been routed, they weren't going to give up. They were gathering an even larger force, and were planning to attack again. Well, with our hero dead, we all knew that this time we wouldn't have a chance, and so they decided that the only thing to do was to go. Which they did, and very quickly, too.'

'So where are they now?' said Hal.

'Miles away, putting as much distance between themselves and the Vemorians as they can. Spreading panic as they go, I expect.'

'Why didn't you go?'

'That dead man. I felt quite sure he was our only hope. We couldn't just ignore what he'd told us. After all, he was the one big piece of magic that had happened here for quite a while.' Lugh shrugged his shoulders. 'I was stupid, though. I should have gone with the rest of them. Just me, alone in the village, a horde of enraged Vemorians massing for another go at the village. What could I do that would make any difference?'

'Cut off that bloke's head for a start,' said Hal. 'You agreed to do that, I think you were idiots not to.'

'I agree,' said Gilly. 'A bargain's a bargain, and he kept his side of it.'

'You're right,' said Lugh. 'But I can't.'

'Why not?'

'I'm a soothsayer. It isn't allowed.'

'If you've lost your powers, does it matter?' asked Gilly.

Lugh shook his head. 'I thought about it, but I just can't do it. Look, you come with me, and I'll show you what I mean.'

Five

THE BODY LAY IN THE SHADE OF THE TREE.
'Wow,' said Gilly.

Hal gave a whistle of disbelief. Lugh hadn't exaggerated; this guy was huge.

'He looks as though he's just sleeping,' said Gilly. 'I mean, he hasn't gone white, or waxy or anything.'

'No, he's dead all right,' said Lugh. 'My uncle checked. No breath, nothing. Still, it is a bit strange, isn't it? And you'd think, in this hot weather, and he's been here since yesterday . . .'

Gilly shuddered.

Hal hummed to himself, the way he always did when he was thinking. 'Gilly, we'll have to do it.'

'Hal, you must be mad. You can't go chopping people's heads off, even if they are dead.'

'If we were back home, I wouldn't dream of doing it. It wouldn't arise, though. You don't see people like this striding around the place, do you?'

'True.'

'Lugh, have you got an axe?'

Lugh's face brightened. 'You mean you'll do it? I . . . Well, I was disappointed when you slipped through. I had called for help, you see; I don't know what I'd expected, another giant from beyond the mountains, I suppose. So when I saw you—'

'You thought you were done for,' said Hal with a grin. 'You were probably right.'

'Think of it as a dissection in biology,' Hal urged Gilly as they approached the body, Hal holding a shining axe, Gilly with a saw which Lugh had thoughtfully provided.

'We don't get to do much on giants,' said Gilly, trying not to swallow too hard. 'This is going to be unspeakable.'

Above them, in the tree, a raven suddenly cawed, making them jump.

'Come for carrion,' said Lugh.

'Better get on with it,' said Hal.

'Ugh,' said Gilly.

'There,' said Hal, rather breathlessly. Then, 'I think I'm going to be sick.'

He rushed to the bushes. A very green Gilly was about to join him, when she heard someone speak.

'What a mess you made of that.'

Gilly rounded on Lugh. 'Oh, very nice, you get us to do your dirty work, and then you criticize.'

'I didn't say a word,' said Lugh. 'It was him.' And he pointed to the head.

A white-faced Hal came out of the bushes, and the three of them looked down at the severed head.

'It spoke,' squeaked Gilly.

'Oh, rubbish,' said Hal.

'She's right,' said Lugh.

The head's lips moved. 'Of course I spoke, you fools. Now hold me upright, it's very uncomfortable like this. We need to get organized.'

The three of them stared at each other, and then jumped to one side as the raven flew down from the tree and stood beside the head. It was extremely large, even for a raven, and very black.

'Do as he says, and make it quick.'

'A talking raven,' said Gilly, awed.

'Yes, and a bossy one, too,' said Hal. 'What have we let ourselves in for?'

'Now, this is what you have to do,' said the head.

'Excuse me,' said Hal indignantly. 'I don't think we have to do anything.'

'Yes, you do, yes, you do,' squawked the raven. 'Do as you're told. No manners, no manners, what a shame, what a shame, what a shame.'

'It isn't a matter of manners,' said Hal crossly. He hated people telling him he had no manners, and he wasn't going to take that from a raven. 'It's just that we – me and my sister – are just visiting here. I gave Lugh a hand with his body problem, but that's it.'

'Oh no it isn't, oh no it isn't, not by any means,' said the raven. 'You touched one of the gods, his blood has fallen on you. There's no getting away from it, no, no, no.'

'What blood?' said Hal.

'He's right,' hissed Gilly. 'There, on your hand, and there's some on your leg.'

Hal looked at it with distaste. 'So what?'

The raven hopped from foot to foot, looking very black and very nasty.

The head gave a great sigh. The kind of sigh adults make when someone young has done something they consider very stupid.

'You're very slow on the uptake,' said the head. 'I don't know where you've come from, but by your age you should have learnt to do what you're told by people in authority.'

'You aren't in authority,' Hal pointed out. 'You aren't in anything. You're just a head. You can talk, but you can't move.'

'Oh yes I can,' said the head. 'I can move quite easily, because you're going to carry me.'

'That's where you're wrong,' said Hal. 'For a start, I can see that even just as a head you're extremely heavy. Besides, I don't make a habit of carrying anybody's head around. It's uncivilized.'

'Hal,' whispered Lugh. 'Be careful. You don't know what you're doing. You have no idea—'

Hal took no notice; he brushed Lugh's warning hand away and folded his arms.

Lugh spoke respectfully to the head. 'Let me speak to my friend here. He's a stranger, he doesn't understand about the gods.'

'Oh, very well,' said the head, clearly not pleased. 'Explain quickly, and then I can tell you what you've got to do.'

'Yes, quickly,' said the raven. 'You Tuans have no sense of urgency, it's no wonder you've got yourselves into this fix. What a shame, what a shame, what a—'

'Oh, shut UP,' said Hal.

Gilly sat on a rock; Hal slouched against a tree.

'OK, Lugh,' said Hal. 'You've explained. Although he's only a head, he's one of the Third Race, he's some kind of god, although not as powerful as some gods are. Because he has this power, we more or less have to do what he tells us. Right?'

'That's it,' said Lugh.

'Fine, but Gilly and I aren't Tuans or Vemorians or

anything to do with you. We're what, visitors? Strangers? Foreigners? Whatever. We don't belong here, we don't want to be here, and we're certainly not getting involved in anything more to do with that gruesome head.'

'It drips,' put in Gilly.

'What drips?' asked Lugh, surprised.

'The head. It's making a gory puddle on the grass. It's disgusting.'

'No problem,' said Lugh. 'We'll put it into a basket with some rushes or something. I'm sure it won't go on dripping.'

'I can't see why it's dripping, anyway,' said Gilly. 'I wouldn't have thought a god would drip at all.'

'The drips aren't the point,' said Hal impatiently. 'He can drip away as much as he likes for all I care. What I want to know is, how do we get out of here?'

'You can't,' said Lugh.

'You mean we're here for good?' said Gilly, appalled, thinking of her parents. The police hunt, the appeals on TV, the hopelessness and despair of her mother and father when they finally realized she and Hal had vanished permanently. 'I thought you said that time was different here.'

'It's simple, Gilly,' Hal interrupted.

'I'm talking,' said Gilly. She hated the way people jumped into the middle of what you were saying.

'You're imagining your parents worrying,' said Lugh. 'Well, there are a lot of worried parents here, too.'

Hal didn't look very impressed with this line of argument, and Lugh went on hastily. 'I don't know how long you'll be here. You could go back to where you've come from in the next ten minutes. It might be ten years. I don't know how much time will have passed where you've come from, all I know is that usually time here isn't time there – and vice versa.'

'Usually?' said Gilly, appalled.

'Usually,' repeated Lugh. 'So while you're here, you have to go on with life as we live it. Life as we live it is rather dangerous just now. That means you can't just sit here and hope you'll be whisked back home.'

'Why not?' said Hal. 'Seems a good enough plan to me.'

Lugh sighed. 'One, because the Vemorians will be here shortly, and they won't leave you sitting under a tree, they'll take you away to sell you in the slave market. Two, that head has plans for all of us, and you don't argue with one of them.'

'Why not?'

'Oh, grow up, Hal,' said Gilly. 'Use *your* head. You can see that nothing's normal here. Lugh belongs here. If he says that's the way things are, then I suppose he's right. Let's find out what the head wants us to do.'

'Good,' said Lugh.

'I shall do what I want,' said Hal. 'Not what some talking head tells me to do.'

Just as though the head was the technology master, Gilly thought gloomily. She had a feeling Hal was in for a shock.

He was.

He found himself propelled through the air, his feet just scraping the surface of the ground. The raven was on his shoulder, her claws digging in, hard, and she was squawking in his ear in a most disagreeable way.

Hal shot forward in front of the head as though someone had given him a very hard shove in the back. He fell on his hands and knees, face to face with the head.

It spoke. 'I've been very tolerant,' it said in a nasty way. 'I can see you and the girl are foreigners, you don't understand our ways. But enough's enough; now you had better start understanding. You have my blood on you, I can make you do whatever I want, as you've just seen. Behave yourself, and I won't need to do that again. Any trouble, and you haven't even seen the beginning of what I can do.'

Lugh helped him to his feet. 'He's right,' he hissed in his ear. 'That's what I was trying to tell you.'

Hal dusted himself down. The head gave him a baleful look, told them to be quiet, although nobody was saying anything, and began to speak in a slow and important way.

'Your task is to carry me to the Walled City of the Tuans. There you must bury me in the ground of the high hill.'

Lugh let out a long, incredulous whistle.

'My raven will accompany us. This raven is a sacred bird, and must be obeyed.'

Hal made a noise which could have meant anything; Gilly knew it was Halspeak for 'I'm not taking orders from a raven'. She frowned at him.

Silence. Lugh cleared his throat. He was nervous, thought Gilly. This is real for him, in a way that it isn't real for us. On the other hand, she reminded herself, it was becoming all too real for her and Hal as well.

'Er,' said Lugh. 'Um. Supposing we can do this—'

The head glared at him.

'I mean, when we've done this,' Lugh amended hastily. 'Um, what then?'

'What then? Why, then you will have completed the task set upon you by the Third Race, and you're free of any further obligation – for the time being,' it added unpleasantly. 'Until we need you again. Oh, and once my head is buried, the Tuans will get back their old skills, which should mean that you will be able to deal with the Vemorians. Always supposing there are any of you left, that is, because the way the Vemorians are mopping you up . . .' His voice was rich with contempt.

Gilly was shocked. 'They aren't planning to wipe all the Tuans out, are they?' she whispered to Lugh.

Lugh kept a wary eye on the talking head, but its attention was taken up by something the raven was murmuring into his ear. 'No, but when they take people captive, they . . . they sort of take them over. Although they're Tuans, they become like Vemorians. They think in a different way, and want to live like Vemorians. It's difficult to explain, because you don't know what the Vemorians are like.'

'And I don't think we want to,' said Hal firmly.

'Unfortunately,' said Lugh, 'if we're going to take this head to the Walled City, we'll have to travel across Vemoria.'

'Oh, terrific,' said Hal. 'We'll be so inconspicuous, with a talking head and a bossy raven!'

'It's going to be tricky,' admitted Lugh. 'Trickier than you know, because although the Vemorians gave up cutting off people's heads a good long while ago, they've got a thing about heads. They have stone ones everywhere, and I think they'd very much like to have a big talking one like him.'

'But he's a god,' said Hal. 'He'll make them do whatever he wants.'

'No, the gods can't control just anyone,' said Lugh patiently. 'The head can make us do what he wants because he came to fight for us, my village, I mean, and because you cut his head off. Those are ties, and they give him power over us. In Vemoria, particularly

without a body, he won't be nearly as powerful –
unless, of course, some of his friends turn up to help
him.'

'Also without heads?' asked Hal.

'No, complete, and then they can be really dangerous,' said Lugh.

'Oh, goody,' said Hal.

Six

'**P**SST!' SAID GILLY.
The other two looked at her.

'The raven's finished bending the head's ear. I think we're going to get our marching orders.'

They were, and they were given in a particularly irritating way. It reminded Hal and Gilly of all the worst people they knew; the ones who criticized and nagged and found fault with you whatever you did, and who treated you as though you had nothing between your ears at all.

'Which, by the time she's finished going on at us, we won't have,' grumbled Gilly.

'A container for the head,' said Hal. 'That's the first thing.'

'A basket,' said Lugh.

'Do you think the head's going to think a basket is grand enough for him?' Gilly asked doubtfully.

Lugh shrugged his shoulders. 'It'll have to be. Nothing else will be big enough, and besides, we'll have to strap him on.'

'Strap him on to what?'

'A donkey,' said Lugh.

Hal gave a snort of laughter. 'Oh, his nibs is going to love that.'

'Cut it out, Hal.' Gilly could see that Lugh was taking all this very seriously.

'I am,' Lugh said gratefully. 'I know it must all seem very weird to you, but it isn't a game, Hal.'

Hal looked unconvinced, but a well-aimed kick from Gilly made him realize that she, too, was taking it seriously.

There was a low laugh from the other side of the fountain. 'Squabbling already?' a voice said.

They whirled round. It was Lugh's witchy aunt.

'Hello, Mab,' said Lugh, with no great enthusiasm. 'I thought you'd left.'

'No, no, I couldn't desert you,' she said. 'I expect you'll need my help.'

Lugh looked even more unenthusiastic. 'Look, Mab, we've got to get to the Walled City. You see, we cut off the giant's head, and—'

'I know, I know.' Mab waved a gracious hand. 'I know what you did, and what the head told you. I'm coming too, to keep an eye on you.'

Lugh looked worried. 'Is that a good idea?'

'Maybe, maybe not,' said the witch in her maddening way. 'Makes no difference, I'm coming. Only don't mention it to that head, if you don't mind.'

Lugh tried again. 'I don't think we need help,' he said.

'Good gracious, I can't let you set off across Vemoria in the company of a decapitated god, an idiotic black bird' – here she gave another sniff – 'and two useless foreigners.'

'If you mean Hal and me,' began Gilly, 'I think—'

'Say no more,' said Mab. 'Lugh, you wanted a basket. Go to your aunt's house, there's that big one outside the back door.'

'That might be big enough,' said Lugh.

'Of course it is, that's why I suggested it. Now, off

you go, take your friends with you, I'll be along in a moment.'

'What are you going to do?' Lugh asked suspiciously.

'Just arrange a few things so that the Vemorians don't find life as comfortable here as they'd like . . .'

'Aunt!' began Lugh.

'Nothing much,' said Mab airily. 'Arrange a plague of flies, turn the water brown, make the drains smell. Nothing serious, but the Vemorians will hate it. Pity there isn't anything more powerful, but I can only do witchy magic. It'll annoy them, just the same,' she added with satisfaction.

Lugh led them back through the village to his house. It was painted a pale blue, and looked very tranquil in the flickering shadows cast by the branches of a broad-leaved tree which grew in front of it.

Inside, it was pleasantly cool, and dim in the shuttered light. Gilly didn't like the signs of flight: household items left lying about, clothes bunched on a chair, drawers hanging open.

Lugh ignored all that and went through to the back of the house. There, as Mab had said, was a big old basket.

'My aunt used it for logs,' he said as he inspected it.

'Don't tell the head that,' advised Gilly.

'By the time we've given it a scrub and filled it with rushes and found something to wrap round him, it'll be just the thing.'

'He should be jolly grateful for anything,' said Hal.

'It can't be very comfortable with your neck stump on the ground like that,' said Gilly. She shuddered. 'I hate to think of it.'

'It isn't really a stump,' said Hal. 'Not in the normal way, because in the normal way, he'd be dead, and that would be the end of it. Anyhow, it's stopped bleeding, didn't you notice?'

'I wasn't looking particularly,' said Gilly with distaste. 'Come on, Lugh, you'll have to scrub harder than that if you're going to make any difference to the basket. How are you going to put it on the donkey?'

In her mind's eye, Gilly could see the basket perched perilously on the donkey's back, swaying and lurching at every reluctant step the animal took.

'On one side, held on with leather straps,' said Lugh. 'I'll show you.'

'Won't you need an equal weight on the other side?' asked Hal.

Lugh nodded. 'Yes, there's a bag which we can sling on the other side. We'll need it for clothes and things.'

'Clothes?' said Gilly. She was feeling more and more despondent; there was a reality about all this which she wasn't at all keen on. Up until now, she had felt it was like a strange dream; just visiting. But now, a journey, packing, clothes . . . Far too real and not at all temporary. 'We don't have any other clothes,' she said.

'No,' said Lugh. 'There are plenty around, I'll find you some. You can't travel dressed as you are, your clothes look very odd.'

Gilly looked doubtfully down at her shorts, they seemed all right to her.

'You'll need a tunic on top,' said Lugh. 'Everyone wears tunics here. And we'll need to take some warmer clothes. It can get cold at night, and in any case, Vemoria is colder than here.'

'Cold?' said Hal. 'Why, it's high summer!'

'Not here, it isn't,' said Lugh. 'It's early autumn.' He

could see from Hal's face that he was going to argue. 'Look at the trees, if you don't believe me. You don't always come through in the same season. And winter comes early in Vemoria, it's a chilly place.'

Gilly took the basket from him and shook it briskly. 'That'll be OK,' she said. 'How long is this journey going to take? Where do we stay – or do we camp?'

Lugh shook his head. 'No camping. We'll be across the border into Vemoria very quickly – unfortunately,' he added. 'We would have been several days away from the old borders, as they were before the Vemorians went on the rampage. Camping is not a Vemorian activity, we'd be arrested at once. No, we'll have to stay at inns and lodging houses along the way.'

Hal looked startled. 'How do we pay?'

'There's money here,' said Lugh. 'My uncle left quite a lot for me to bring with me when I came, he thought it was wiser to split it up, in case they got robbed on the way. There's a lot of robbery at the moment, with so many people trying to get away from the Vemorians. I'll see to that, while you line the basket with rushes.'

Gilly wasn't at all sure what rushes looked like. 'We don't have much call for them where we come from,' she explained to Lugh.

'You used to have them strewn on the floor.'

'Centuries ago,' said Hal.

'Useful to know about them, then,' said Lugh helpfully. 'In case you find yourself back in those times.'

'Don't,' said Gilly, pushing aside the thought of the rooms at home, rush-free, definitely belonging to the late twentieth century – and a world away.

Lugh raised an eyebrow at her. 'Try to live only in

the present moment,' he advised. 'You'll find it easier. I'll get you some rushes.'

'There,' said Hal, putting in a final layer of rushes and sitting back on his heels. 'That'll have to do, and if it isn't good enough for him, that's just too bad.'

'He can't complain,' said Gilly. 'It's all lined, nice and cosy for him.'

'Good,' said Lugh. 'He wants something smooth to go round him,' he went on. 'Velvet, silk, something like that. I don't know where I'm going to find that.'

'No problem,' said Mab, suddenly materializing by the side of a big chest of drawers. 'Take this.'

Lugh looked at the piece of material which Mab was holding out. 'That's my aunt's,' he said doubtfully. 'My other aunt,' he added, for Gilly's benefit. 'My uncle's wife, not his sister, who's my mother's sister . . . oh, never mind. She left with all the others.' He turned to Mab. 'She won't want me to use this, you don't know what I want it for.'

The witch snorted. 'Of course I know what you want it for. You just take it. If she wanted to be fussy, she should have taken it with her – and in any case, she and your uncle shouldn't have left like that without you. Although I will say this for your uncle, he did say they must find you and take you with them. Your aunt wouldn't have that, she just wanted to get her own precious self away to safety. Typical! She couldn't give a *that*' – and she gave a most impressive snap of her fingers – 'for anyone else.' She sniffed. 'Besides, it's a loathsome colour, and your aunt looks dreadful in any shade of green, let alone that one.'

Gilly and Hal watched Lugh putting a halter on the rather bad-tempered looking donkey which was the only one that had been left behind. It had such a terrible reputation that the fleeing villagers had agreed it could be their parting gift to the Vemorians. Lugh let out a squeal as the donkey butted him in the stomach, and then stamped on his feet with its hard little hooves.

'You could help,' Lugh called reproachfully.

Hal slid down from the fence which he had been sitting on. Thinking hard, from what Gilly knew of him. He sidled over to the donkey, uttering soothing noises, and then, when he got near it, gave it a hefty biff on the rump. The donkey was so surprised that it shot in the air, and before it could get its bearing again so as to have a good go at Hal, Lugh had the halter on.

The donkey bared its teeth and dug all its hooves in.

'I don't think this is going to work,' Gilly told Lugh.

'It's got to,' said Lugh, breathless with tugging. 'Have you any idea how heavy that head is? We couldn't carry it half a mile. No, we've got to use the donkey.'

Hal picked up a long twig, and with Lugh pulling at the halter and Hal prodding its rump, the donkey finally deigned to move.

There was a flap and creak of wings, and the raven flew down. 'Come along, come along,' she said in irritated tones. 'No time to waste, no time to waste.'

'The donkey doesn't want to come,' said Lugh.

'Huh,' said the raven. She swooped into the air and landed with a satisfying thump on the donkey's back. She jiggled her claws. 'Move,' she cawed.

The donkey moved.

The head could hardly dance with impatience, but it was clear from his expression that if he'd had a body, he would have danced.

'We've been finding a basket, and catching the donkey to carry it,' explained Lugh, dumping the basket on the ground beside the head.

'A log basket,' the head said at once. 'And I won't travel on a donkey. You can carry me.'

'Quite right, quite right too,' put in the raven. 'A donkey, indeed! For a god! What are you thinking of, what are you thinking of?'

'It's the donkey or nothing,' said Hal. 'And you can glue my feet to the ground or make me rush where I don't want to go like you did before, but you can't make any of us strong enough to carry you on a long journey.'

'You can each take a handle,' said the head sulkily.

'Still too heavy,' said Lugh.

'Besides,' said Gilly, 'you'd feel seasick, swinging to and fro. And what if one of us stumbled or tripped while we were carrying you? Hal's always tripping over his feet.'

'Thanks,' said Hal under his breath.

Gilly glared at him, she wasn't making nasty remarks about his feet, which were very big, she was simply pointing out a fact which might make the donkey more attractive to the head. 'Just trying to help,' she muttered.

'Disgraceful, disgraceful,' cawed the raven. 'Come along now, come along. We have to be on our way.'

'We can't leave just yet,' said Lugh. 'I have to ask someone about our route.'

'I will tell you the way,' said the head grandly.

'I'm your guide, you idiotic boy,' said the raven. 'You don't need to ask anyone else; I know where we're going.'

'I need hot tips about the best way to go and where the trouble spots are,' said Lugh, holding his ground.

'I thought everyone had left,' said Hal in an aside to Lugh.

It had come as rather a shock when he realized that for the first time in his life, there were no adults to turn to for help or advice. True, when the adults were about, he preferred to go his own way and not to take any advice if he could help it, but even he had to admit that he would appreciate his mother or father going along on this particular trip.

'There's always Lugh's auntie,' Gilly pointed out.

'I don't think she qualifies as an adult,' said Hal. 'She's a witch, she never looks the same two appearances running, and she comes and goes like a puff of smoke.'

'I know a shepherd,' said Lugh. 'He won't have gone, he'll hide his sheep in caves where the Vemorians will never find them. He knows the countryside around here like the back of his hand. And he'll know where the Vemorians are right now. We don't want to set off and run straight into them.'

'I'll go with Lugh,' said Hal.

'You aren't going anywhere,' said the head, evilly. 'You must think I was born yesterday if you expect me to let all three of you wander off.'

'You'd better stay here and sort out some food with Gilly and my aunt,' said Lugh.

'Does the head eat?' said Gilly, very softly.

'No,' said Lugh. 'Not our sort of food, anyhow. And while he's in his present state, I shouldn't think he'll eat or drink at all.'

'Thank goodness,' said Gilly, who didn't care for the idea of having to feed the head.

'Where is your aunt?' said Hal.

'Around,' said Lugh. 'Call her when you're out of

sight of those two. She doesn't like the gods, and she certainly isn't keen on talking ravens.'

'Get going, get going,' said the raven malevolently. 'You're very slow, slow-witted and slow-footed. What a shame, what a shame, what a shame!'

'I hate that raven,' said Gilly. Wasn't it typical? Even when you'd been transported through a time warp, or into another reality or whatever had happened to them, you didn't get away from people who ordered you around and felt free to criticize you all the time.

'People are bad enough,' said Hal gloomily. 'But a raven!'

Seven

*P*UTTING THE HEAD IN THE BASKET HAD BEEN A nasty job. It was so big and felt so warm and firm and alive, they found it difficult to believe that it stopped at the neck.

He had been critical of their handling, too. 'Clumsy idiots, you're pulling my hair. Put me down very, very gently, because otherwise I might lose my temper, and you wouldn't like that at all.'

'Not at all, not at all,' echoed the raven gleefully.

Hal's face had a mutinous look as he set about looking for food in the kitchen of Lugh's house. 'Probably riddled with germs,' he said. 'No fridge, no freezer . . .'

'If you want fresh food,' said a voice in his ear, 'you'd better try the ice house.'

'Oh, it's you,' said Hal, eyeing Mab in some astonishment. She was dressed as an air stewardess, complete with scarf, bag and smile.

'Don't you like it?' she said.

Gilly came into the kitchen with an armful of clothes. 'Hal, these should fit you,' she began. Then she saw Lugh's aunt and stared, stunned into silence.

Mab gave a twirl. 'My travel garb,' she said. Then, seeing the expressions on their faces, she frowned. 'Why are you staring? Haven't I got it right? Isn't this what you wear in your country when you travel?'

'Not exactly,' said Gilly.

'No way,' said Hal.

'Shut up, Hal,' said Gilly, who had taken rather a liking to Lugh's aunt. 'Only air stewardesses wear those clothes. It's a uniform. For when they fly. In planes.'

'I know what planes are,' said Mab, plainly annoyed. 'Do you think we only know about broomsticks here? I've seen pictures, I'm sure you're wrong.'

'We aren't,' said Hal. 'And if we're trying not to attract attention, I don't think that outfit is going to help.'

'Oh, very well,' said the witch, turning with a blur back into her more normal self, although Gilly wasn't really sure what her normal self was.

Mab became efficient. 'I'll see to the food,' she said. 'You,' and she pointed to Hal, 'can take those water bottles and fill them from the fountain. That's the best water there is, because you don't know how near the Vemorians are to us now, or whether they've tampered with the water supply.'

Hal stared at her. 'How do you know that the water in the fountain is all right?'

'It comes from a well, there's no way they could have contaminated that with their evil potions.'

'Hang on, you were going to turn the water brown.'

'I have, but not the fountain – yet.'

As Hal left the house, a large water bottle in each hand, he came face to face with the raven. It was perched on a post near the door, flapping its wings in an unpleasant way. 'Where do you think you're going?'

'To the fountain,' said Hal, holding up the water bottles. 'OK with you?'

'As long as I can see you,' replied the raven. 'Hurry up, hurry up, this is all taking far too long, far too long.'

She'll give me a black mark in a minute, Hal said to himself as he hung over the edge of the fountain to catch the stream of water.

Lugh came back down the hill, looking thoughtful. He winked at Hal as he helped him tighten the straps which held the baskets on the donkey's back.

'Did you find the shepherd?' whispered Hal.

Lugh nodded. 'He's given me some good advice,' he said, keeping a sharp eye on the raven. It was watching them with cold black eyes as it edged nearer along the rail of the fence.

'This way,' said Lugh confidently, as he tugged at the donkey.

'We should go due north,' the head said.

'No, apparently the Vemorians are massing that way, waiting for people who are trying to escape. If we go this way, and take a path through the Wild Forest, then we should avoid them.'

Gilly didn't altogether like the sound of the Wild Forest. Nor did Mab, who materialized at the rear of their little train, shaking her head. 'The boy's mad, we never go into the Wild Forest,' she said.

'I think he knows what he's doing,' said Hal. 'He's got a plan.'

'I've got a plan, too,' said Gilly. 'Let's get away from all this, and somehow find our way back to the castle, and to the normal world.'

Now it was Mab's turn to shake her head. 'You can't do that. The more you look for a way back, the less likely it is that you'll find it. Just when you least expect it, that's when you'll find yourself sliding through to your own world.'

'When?' said Gilly.

'Could be tomorrow. Could be in five years. Could be never if the Vemorians get hold of you.'

'Thanks,' said Gilly. She wanted to be sitting in her garden at home, warm in the August sun, painting. Or lying on her back in the Hollingsworths' open-air pool. Or in Hal's hammock, reading.

Anywhere, except setting off on a journey through a country she didn't know, to a place she had never heard of, in the company of a talking head, a bossy raven and a not-very-helpful witch.

The small party made their way through the deserted village, pausing by the fountain for the head to be adjusted in the basket so that it could see out. None of them liked walking ahead; those blazing green eyes boring into your back didn't make for comfort. Someone had to lead the donkey, though, so Lugh went first, tugging at the donkey's bridle and making encouraging clicking noises. Hal and Gilly brought up the rear, giving the donkey an occasional thump to encourage it to move more quickly.

Lugh opened a gate; beyond it, a path wound its way up the hill. It all seemed open and quite bare, with only the odd tree here and there. The hillside was thick with bracken, and Gilly could see fat, woolly sheep grazing in an unconcerned way. It seemed rural and peaceful, a pleasant walk on a summer's day.

The raven's voice rang out, bringing her down to earth. 'Keep up at the back there, keep up!'

'Just like a school outing,' grumbled Hal.

'Much, much worse,' said Gilly. 'At least then you

know there's an end to it. Where's the end to this journey?'

'Many journeys have no end,' announced a voice behind them.

'Hello, Mab,' said Gilly. 'I thought you were going to lie low until we got to the forest.'

'I'm trying,' said Mab. 'But I'm not having a lot of luck with my spells just at present. I tried to become an owl, to flit ahead and sit on a branch to welcome you, you understand.'

'And?' said Gilly.

'Fox,' said Mab gloomily. 'I became a fox, only perched on a high branch of a tree in the middle of a field, with all those sheep laughing at me. Hopeless. I don't know what's come over my spells, they're all going wrong.'

'What did you do?' asked Gilly, who couldn't help laughing.

'Turned back into myself and climbed down,' said Mab.

'Where is this forest?' said Hal, putting a hand up to shield his eyes from the sun. 'I can't see anything like a forest for miles around.'

'Wait until we get over this next crest,' said Mab. 'Then you'll see it.'

They trudged on – and on, and on. It was very hot, and they felt none of the spirit of an outing or an adventure that would have made the heat and the walk enjoyable. The raven had taken up a position balanced on the donkey's back where she could talk to the head. The donkey wasn't keen, and became even slower and more reluctant to move.

Hal broke off a small, wiry branch and gave the

donkey a whack across its backside. The donkey bared its teeth, stopped, put its head down, and kicked out, hard.

Hal leapt backwards, sending Mab flying. The raven flew up into the air, cawing furiously. Lugh, his arm nearly wrenched out of its socket by the donkey, which was very strong for its size, tried to calm the animal down. The head rose several inches above the top of the basket and uttered some strange words, making Lugh go pale. The witch, hearing them, immediately vanished again.

'Sorry,' said Hal. 'Just thought I'd try and speed things up a bit.'

'Well, don't,' said Lugh. 'The head nearly wished us all into the lost realms, and if you think it's going to be hard getting out of this fix, then I can tell you, we'd all be lost. For good.'

'Lost realms,' muttered Hal to himself as the raven circled angrily above his head.

'Yes, the lost realms,' screeched the raven as she landed on the donkey's rump, sending up a little cloud of dust. 'The lost realms, you silly boy. I warn you, don't play silly games with a god!'

'Silly games?' said Hal indignantly. 'Look, all I was trying to do was—'

'Shut up, Hal,' said Gilly. 'I think the best thing we can do is to keep a very, very low profile. Just like you do at school when you know you're about to land yourself in dead trouble. OK?'

'I suppose so,' said Hal grudgingly. 'I hate having no control over what I do or how or when—'

'Tough,' said Gilly.

Hal wasn't listening to her. They had reached the top

of the crest, and there, laid out beneath them, was another world. The dry fields gave way to rich green hillsides, leading down to a silvery river which snaked its way across the landscape as far as the eye could see. It sparkled in the sun, and with the meadows along one side of its banks, it looked idyllic.

'Aha,' said Hal.

On the other side of the river, it wasn't idyllic at all. There was a kind of dyke, with coarse grass growing here and there, and beyond that what seemed like miles of flat nothingness.

'It's a swamp,' said Hal at last.

'A *black* swamp,' said Gilly.

They could make out sluggish streams of dark-coloured water which criss-crossed the dark, desolate terrain.

'Like Avernus,' said Hal thoughtfully and without enthusiasm.

'Um, yes,' said Gilly. 'The black lake which the Romans believed was an entrance to the underworld.'

'That's the one,' said Hal. 'No birds would fly over it.'

Gilly sighed. 'No, and if it looked like that other side of the river, you can see why. Bet the raven will fly over it, looks like its spiritual home.'

Lugh turned round to call to them. 'The Wild Forest,' he said, gesturing towards the dark forest beyond the swamp, which stretched away towards the horizon.

'You mean we're going to go through that?' said Gilly, appalled. 'Across the swamp and through that forest?'

'Sorry,' said Lugh, 'but, yes, we have to. It takes us a long way into Vemoria, but we aren't likely to meet many Vemorians on our way. They don't like the Wild Forest.'

'No,' said Hal. 'I can see that it wouldn't be anyone's first choice for a day out in the woods.'

'Come along, come along,' said the raven. 'This isn't a holiday outing, you know, we have to get on, we have to get on.'

'Just a minute,' said Hal. 'Lugh, it's going to take us days to get through that, if we don't get lost after about ten minutes in any case. What are we going to do when it gets dark?'

'It'll only take a few hours to get across the swamp,' said Lugh helpfully. 'And darkness isn't actually a problem in the Wild Forest. You'll see. And there are places where we can sleep.'

He looked at the expressions on Gilly's and Hal's faces, and sighed. 'I'm sorry,' he said. 'It seems hopeless, I know, but it really is the best way. Trust me.'

'Of course we trust you,' Gilly said quickly. 'It's just a bit of a surprise.'

Hal was looking again at the forest. 'It's very strange,' he said at last. 'You'd think it had been planted rather than growing naturally. It's almost as though it were a maze.'

'That's what it is!' cried Mab, materializing suddenly at Hal's shoulder and making him jump. 'That's exactly what it is, a maze. And what happens to people who go into mazes?'

'They get lost, if it's me,' said Gilly.

'Exactly,' said the witch.

Eight

I'LL NEVER FORGET THIS SWAMP, THOUGHT Gilly. Nothing can ever be as bad as this.

'I wish you were right,' said Lugh.

Hal lifted his eyes from his feet and glared at Lugh. 'Can't you tell? Can't you see any further forward than the next slimy tuft?'

'I can see far enough ahead to see worse danger than this,' said Lugh sombrely.

'Danger!' said Hal. 'Danger's exciting. This is just plain hell.'

'We haven't got to the forest yet,' said Lugh with foreboding.

Gilly didn't have a thought beyond the slimy, sucking, stinking black mud under their feet. There was no danger of sinking into the mud, the ground just beneath it was solid enough. It was the heavy, fetid air coming up from the mud. It was the sinister gulping noises which the mud made – not only where they were walking but, inexplicably, a few feet away from them. It was the creatures buzzing around their heads.

'These horrible insects,' said Hal, taking a swipe at a thick, blue-black one which looked rather like a giant mosquito.

The insects hummed around them, skimming over the muddy surface, rising into the air and then zooming down at them. These weren't the cheerful sounds of bees clustered around flowers, or crickets clicking on a summer evening. No, these were the kind of insect sounds that you might hear in your worst dreams.

Gilly raised her head and looked longingly towards the dark line which marked the edge of the forest. It never seemed to get any nearer, though Lugh, turning his head round from his place by the donkey, assured her that they were doing very well, making good time.

The donkey looked like Hal and Gilly felt. Its head was down, its tail swished uncomfortably from side to side, its eyes were half-closed to keep out the insects that droned around them and clung to its eyelashes.

On, and on. One foot, then another. Their feet felt as though they were going to dissolve in the mud, would never be clean and dry again. Both Hal and Gilly had slipped more than once, and had damp, evil-smelling mud caked on their legs and arms and clothes.

'Not far now,' said Lugh. 'Not far.'

Numb, Gilly looked through aching eyes to see the first straggling plants that marked the end of the swamp and the beginning of the forest. She managed a weak smile, and wondered if she looked as exhausted as Hal and Lugh.

They struggled up the slight incline that led from the crusted, decaying edges of the swamp. Ahead were huge trees; motionless, but green and alive. Gilly was overcome with relief.

'We made it,' she said.

Hal said nothing, but threw himself on the ground and lay there, with his eyes shut and his arms stretched out from his sides. Gilly sank down beside him, wrapping her arms round her legs and resting her head on her knees. The donkey stood a little way off, flanks heaving.

The raven was as fresh as a daisy. 'No time to stop, no time to rest, we must get on, we must get on.'

They took no notice.

'No time to be tired, what a shame, what a shame, what a shame.'

The head, who had had the best of the journey, was also not in a mood to hang about.

'It is not the place of servants to be tired and give up and rest when they want to,' he stated.

'Servant yourself,' muttered Hal without opening his eyes.

'I can make you move, and I will.'

Lugh cleared his throat. 'Better not,' he said. 'They've already come a long way today, from another world in fact. If they don't rest and eat, they won't be able to complete the journey. And I can't manage on my own.'

'Oh, very well,' said the head impatiently. 'A short rest, and then we continue our journey.'

'I've had enough of this journey already,' murmured Gilly.

'Get your breath back,' said Lugh, 'and then we'll make a move.' He lowered his voice. 'Don't worry about the head if he tries to bully you to go on. He doesn't have his full powers in the forest, there's too much other magic about.'

'What are you saying, why are you whispering?' demanded the raven, hopping from foot to foot.

'I'm just pointing out that the sooner we get into the forest, the sooner we'll get through it,' said Lugh in his normal voice.

'True, true.'

'And how long will that take?' said Hal.

'I don't know,' said Lugh. 'It's a funny place. It could take days – or hours. I think we'll have to find somewhere safe to spend the night, then tomorrow, with luck—'

'With luck?' said Hal suspiciously.

'I'm sure we'll get through fairly quickly,' said Lugh.

It was as though they had walked into night; into a thick, heavy, breathing darkness, which made Hal and Gilly feel cold.

'Not just any coldness,' said Gilly, 'but that awful fingery coldness that starts at your neck and works its way down your spine.'

'Yes,' said Hal. He remembered the feeling, and remembered also that it only came at the very worst moments of your life.

'Is this the Wild Forest?' said Gilly in despair. 'Is it like this all the way? How can we ever get through it?'

Lugh's voice came out of the gloom. 'It seems terrible at first,' he said encouragingly. 'Your eyes will get used to it soon, and then you'll find you can see a bit.'

'There's no light at all,' said Hal, looking upwards to where the branches of the tall trees grew and intertwined so thickly that no daylight could ever penetrate.

'No sunlight, no,' said Lugh. 'But the trees and ground have their own light. Just wait.'

Although at first the wood had seemed silent, they now began to realize that it wasn't.

Not at all.

Better if it had been.

There were scuttlings and dull thumps and

unearthly cries and screams and screeches. An owl – or was it an owl? – hooted eerily. A howling noise seemed to come from above their heads; something crunched and whooped in the undergrowth over to one side of them.

'That raven should feel at home here,' muttered Hal, bumping into the donkey, who took the opportunity to give him a quick nip with its strong teeth.

'Quiet,' commanded the head. 'We have come the wrong way. It was very unwise of you, boy, to bring us here.'

'It isn't the wrong way,' said Lugh. 'We can get through the forest, there is a way. If we had gone over the hills along the normal paths, the Vemorians would have jumped on us at once.'

Hal shrugged, although nobody could see him doing it. 'What's the difference?' he said. 'Now, or later, they'll get hold of us. Get it over with, I say.'

'Don't be so feeble,' said Gilly. 'No, I didn't mean that, you don't think this is a good idea, and nor do I, but Lugh's right, they won't find us here.'

'No,' continued Lugh. 'And we should come out well inside Vemoria, where nobody will be on guard or watching out for stray Tuans. We'll be just another set of foreigners travelling to the capital. Lots do.'

'Oh yes?' said Hal. 'Complete with a decapitated god-head and a talking raven?'

'Maybe not exactly,' said Lugh.

'I should stop arguing and start moving,' said Mab, arriving in the middle of the path and making them all jump.

'Mab,' said Gilly, very pleased to see her. 'I thought you'd stayed behind.'

'No, but catch me coming across that swamp, ugh!

Fortunately, I have other ways of getting about. Mind you, I think I should have given this place a miss. I had no idea it was so bad.'

'Haven't you been here before?'

Mab shook her head. 'This is no place for witches, I feel it in my blood. And it's so dark.'

In fact, Lugh was right. Gradually they were able to see a little. The trees and plants and even the moss-like growths on the ground seemed to give off a strange glow. Not much, but coming from so many sources . . .

'It's like that blue light-bulb which stays on overnight if you're in a sleeper on a train,' whispered Gilly.

'Eerie,' agreed Hal.

'Enough to see by,' said Lugh.

'No problem, no problem at all,' said the raven.

'I hate birds,' said Mab, with feeling.

'Move,' said the raven.

They moved.

There was, despite the sounds, a vast stillness hanging over the forest. The air was heavy and dank, and, as they moved away from the swamp, it was getting hotter and hotter. Not a warm, welcoming natural heat; no, this was a brooding oppressive, clammy heat.

'Jungly,' said Hal.

'It is jungle, really,' said Gilly. 'It's not like a wood at all.'

As their eyes gradually became accustomed to the strange light, they could make out the leaves and great hanging tendrils of the plants which grew to make the impenetrable canopy above them. Stalks thicker than tree trunks, leaves two and three feet across. Plants with evil-looking spikes at their heart, climbers winding round towering trees as though they were strangling them.

'Which they probably are,' said Hal, as they came into a small clearing.

'I think we should stop,' said Lugh.

He ignored the roar of protest from the head and the flapping flurry of wings and loud squawks from the raven.

'We need to eat and sleep,' said Lugh. 'We don't know when we'll come to another place like this.'

Gilly couldn't imagine anywhere worse to spend the night.

Lugh gave a thin smile. 'I know, it's pretty bad. But the raven and the donkey will warn us if anything comes too close. And we need to eat, I'm hungry.'

They all were, and were glad to sit down and eat the food which Mab had packed for them. Mab herself had vanished again. 'She doesn't like being too close to the head,' Lugh whispered to Hal and Gilly.

Hal, although he felt drained of energy, didn't feel safe in the clearing.

'We aren't safe anywhere,' said Lugh. 'But I think we'll get through the night.'

'How will we know when it's dawn?' said Gilly.

'By the cold,' Lugh replied.

'The cold?' said Gilly in surprise. 'What cold?'

They wrapped themselves in blankets before lying down on the hard, unpleasant ground.

'Cold, indeed,' said Gilly, dripping with sweat.

'Let's just hope we aren't attacked,' said Hal in gloomy tones.

They were attacked all right, as the insects which they thought they had left behind in the swamp came swarming out of the forest. They pounced on the blanketed figures with roars and buzzes and whines. Hal and Gilly beat about them with their arms at the high-pitched shrieks, until Lugh showed them that they had to let the insects land on them . . .

'I can't,' said Gilly. 'It's revolting.'

. . . and then squash them with their thumbs.

'Which is even more revolting,' said Hal, trying it.

None of them got much sleep, and Gilly felt that she had only just dozed off when a terrible cold crept into the air.

'Did you ask what cold?' said Hal from under his blanket. 'Now you know.'

Nine

SHIVERING AND YAWNING, THEY GOT TO THEIR feet. The donkey looked distinctly unhappy, and Gilly went over to give it a friendly pat.

Nip.

'The donkey bit me,' said Gilly indignantly. 'I was only trying to be kind.'

'Waste of time,' said Lugh. 'It only likes other donkeys. It bites anything else that moves and that it can catch.'

The raven eyed the donkey a little warily when she heard that, and hopped back on to its perch on the donkey's rump.

'Load the head, load the head,' she cawed. 'Right away, you're very slow, what a shame, what a shame, what a shame.'

'Pity something didn't come out of the forest and get that raven,' said Hal.

'Sssh,' said Lugh, looking round the clearing. 'I think we go that way,' he said, pointing to a narrow path just visible through the undergrowth.

'Are you sure?' said Hal doubtfully. 'I mean, I don't want to be rude, but do you have any idea of the way?'

'The head should know,' said Gilly. 'Being a god. Or part of a god, anyway.'

Even though they were only able to see the top of the god's head and the fierce eyes looking through the gap in the basket, they were able to tell that he was frowning.

'Not in here,' he said. 'This is a completely wild place, beyond my powers. Beyond your magic, too,' he added, glaring at Lugh.

'Me?' said Lugh mildly. 'I lost my magic some time ago.'

'Lugh doesn't look terribly worried,' Gilly said to Hal in a whisper.

'I imagine he's beyond worrying,' replied Hal.

Gilly shivered. 'I hate this forest. It's ancient and terrible. Do you suppose there are wild animals in it? Tigers?'

'And alligators,' said Hal, not looking very happy at the thought.

'Traffic wardens,' said Mab, popping up behind them and startling them all.

Gilly and Hal stared at her. 'Traffic wardens?'

'Isn't that what you're most afraid of, where you come from? I never heard of anyone complaining about wild animals. Tigers and alligators, no. Traffic wardens, yes, all the time.'

Hal laughed. 'I don't think this is the right habitat for a traffic warden.'

'Good,' said Mab. 'There's one thing we don't have to be afraid of, then. What do they look like?'

'Well,' Gilly began.

'No,' said Hal. 'It would take too long to explain. Never mind about traffic wardens, let's concentrate on getting out of this forest.'

'Getting out of it's easy,' said Mab. 'It's getting *through* it that's the problem.'

'We don't know which path we came by,' explained Gilly.

'Oh, I do,' said Mab. 'That one.'

—— 74 ——

'How can you tell? It looks the same as all the others.'

'It's been trodden on recently,' said Mab.

Lugh came to join them, yanking the donkey's head round with him. 'I daren't let go, because you can bet it'd be off at once, and then we'd be for it.'

'Mab says we came in that way,' said Gilly pointing. 'She says it looks walked-on.'

'Could be,' said Lugh doubtfully. 'Auntie, you aren't making this up, are you?'

Mab shook her head. 'No. I'm not in the mood for jokes, not with Buster there staring at us.'

The raven, who had been sitting on the donkey's back with one eye closed, now came back to life.

'If we came in on that path,' she said, gesturing with a jet black wing, 'then we need to go along that path there. The one on the right. Off we go!'

'I think,' said Lugh, 'that the path we should take is that one, opposite us.'

'No, no, nonsense, nonsense,' squawked the raven.

'Why?' said Mab and Hal together.

Gilly was watching Lugh carefully. 'He knows something we don't,' she said.

'The shepherd told me,' Lugh explained. 'If we came in there, then we take the path straight ahead.'

'If we take the wrong one now, then presumably we're lost,' said Hal.

'No, probably not,' said Mab. 'Most likely, if we get it wrong, we'll end up back where we started.'

'The one on the right,' cried the raven. 'The one on the right, on the right.'

'I still think it's the other one,' said Lugh under his breath as he dragged the donkey round. 'We'll soon find out. And stick to the path. The forest's a dangerous place.'

The path got narrower and narrower, and more difficult to walk along. Then it gave a sudden twist . . .

. . . and they were back in the clearing.

'Stupid, stupid,' hissed the raven. 'Stupid amateur spells.'

Mab tsk-tsked with disapproval. 'Speaking as a professional,' she said, 'whatever else the magic in this wood may be, it's not amateur. It's powerful, it's dark, and I think it's fairly nasty.'

'Don't,' said Gilly with a shudder. 'I already have this feeling that I'm being watched.'

'By animals, do you think?' said Hal, as the party set off again, this time taking the seventh path from the left. 'I have the same feeling, but I don't know what's watching.'

'People live in the Wild Forest,' said Lugh from his post at the donkey's head. He would much rather have walked behind with the others, but he had no choice, someone had to lead the donkey, and he knew the animal best.

'When I say people,' he explained, 'I don't mean like us. They aren't exactly like other people. Well, they wouldn't be, not after generations of being born and bred in the forest. Their eyes are different, they can't leave the forest, the light would blind them.'

'Do they mind outsiders going through their territory?' enquired Hal.

'They hate it,' said Lugh. 'But they can't touch us as long as we keep to the paths. There's some sort of magic in the old ways through the forest, and the forest people can't break it. That's why they hate travellers so much. So don't, whatever you do, wander off the path.'

'I wasn't going to,' said Gilly.

'Do they watch you?' asked Hal.

'All the time,' said Lugh.

'They're tracking us now,' said Mab. 'I can tell. They're moving along parallel to us, only a few feet away, just off the path. Lugh's right, stay on the path. They'll try to get us off, they make noises like people or animals crying out for help, or they play strange music to distract you. That's what people say.'

'What happens if they do catch you?' said Hal.

'They take no prisoners,' said Lugh.

'I don't like this,' said Gilly. 'I don't want to be here.'

'Nor do I,' said Hal. 'I don't think we've got much choice, though. Lugh,' he called out. 'We're coming to a fork. What happens now?'

'We take the left-hand path,' said Lugh. 'The next fork is left as well, and then right. Then two lefts again. We should come to another clearing after a while, and then we can have a pause, have some breakfast.'

'No time to stop, no time to stop!' cawed the raven.

'Of course we'll have to stop,' said Lugh impatiently. 'It's all right for you, just travelling along on the donkey's back, but we're on foot and we're going to get tired. Besides, we have to eat.'

'You should not be tired in the service of the gods,' said the head from its basket.

'No gods of mine,' said Hal at once.

'You are subject to my power, willingly or unwillingly,' said the head firmly. 'The sooner you accept that, the better for all of you.'

'It's ridiculous,' said Hal furiously, kicking a branch out of the way.

'Don't do that!' cried Mab in warning.

Too late. The branch lifted itself up on an enormous number of legs, glared at Hal with two venomous red eyes and made straight for him.

Lugh let go of the donkey, and with one quick

movement picked up a large stone which was lying on the path and hurled it at the creature.

'Get back,' he shouted to Hal, who was staring at the flat, snarling face of his attacker.

The animal gave a horrible, rasping shriek and slunk into the bushes at the side, leaving a very shaken Hal in possession of the path.

'Thank you, Lugh,' said Hal with real feeling. 'I don't know what that was, or what it was planning to do to me, but I didn't like the look of it at all.'

'It would have dug its fangs into you and drunk your blood,' said Mab brutally. 'Not just a mouthful, either, but a couple of pints if you were lucky, and a lot more if you weren't.'

Gilly went an even paler shade of pale. Mab draped an arm across her shoulders and gave her a hug.

'Nothing happened,' she said. 'Hal's all right, so are we all.'

'But we might have been—'

'Might have been! Might have been!' said Mab with immense scorn. 'We haven't got time to worry about might-have-beens, not if we're going to get out of this forest safe and sound.'

Hal, getting his breath back after the shock of the attack, looked at Lugh. 'Thanks,' he said again. 'That was a terrific shot.'

Lugh grinned. 'You were lucky, my aim's not usually that good. Now, we need to get moving, in case Harry there has merely nipped away to gather a few friends.'

His voice trailed into silence as he looked down the path to where he had left the donkey.

No donkey.

No raven.

No head.

Ten

'WE MUST GO AFTER THEM, SAID LUGH IMME-
diately. 'I think they went this way, I'm sure I
can hear them . . .' He paused, listening.

Then, like a flash he was off.

Gilly lunged forward to go after him, but Hal held
her back.

'Wait,' he said.

'The longer we wait, the further away they'll be, and
the less chance we'll have of finding them.'

'So much the better,' said Hal.

He had a stubborn look on his face that Gilly knew
well. So did his parents and his teachers. There was no
reasoning with Hal when he looked like that.

'So?' she said.

'I'm sure there must be a way out of here. Out, back
to our own world, I mean.'

'Don't you want to help Lugh?'

'I don't mind helping Lugh, it's helping that
disgusting head that I object to.'

'We have to help the head to help Lugh.'

'That's what the head says. I don't believe a word of
it. Why should he help Lugh? Once he's got what he
wants, he won't give a toss about Lugh or the rest of
the Tuans.'

Gilly liked to trust people, but she knew that Hal was
shrewd about people in a way that she wasn't. He

always seemed to know which of her friends were OK and which weren't, and he was usually right about adults as well.

'So what do you suggest?'

'We scarper.'

'Where to?' Gilly looked around the dark, enclosing trees, the narrow paths and the unimaginable dangers which lurked if you stepped off them.

'Back the way we came. Maybe the Vemorians are pouring into the villages, maybe they aren't. We didn't see any sign of them, did we? And they can't move that fast. They haven't got tanks or anything like that, it's all footwork here.'

'Then what?'

'Then back to that stone archway, tomb entrance, whatever it is, and see whether we can't slip back.'

Gilly had her doubts. 'Back through the swamp? That's a dreadful idea.'

'It wasn't that bad,' said Hal hopefully.

Gilly wasn't listening. Hal swung round to see what she was looking at. He stiffened, although the tall man approaching seemed normal enough.

'At least he hasn't got a hundred legs and fangs,' whispered Gilly.

The man greeted them courteously, raising his hand in a friendly gesture. Hal, his mouth set, said nothing.

He's blind in one eye, thought Gilly, noticing that whereas one was a clear blue, the other was cloudy and unfocussed.

'Yes, the Vemorians blinded me in one eye. When I was a child,' the man said. 'You're lost.'

'Not exactly,' said Hal rather too quickly. 'I know which way we came into the forest, and we can go back when we want to.'

'Of course,' the man said. 'A strange journey: into a forest, and then back the way you've come.'

'Can you tell us another way out?' said Gilly.

Hal glared at her.

'Oh, there are many ways out. It depends on where you want to go.'

'We don't want to go anywhere, actually,' Hal said. 'Not here. We want to go back where we came from, to our own country.'

'Yes, you're visitors, aren't you? Earth people.'

'Earth people?' That alarmed Gilly. 'This is Earth, too, isn't it? I mean we aren't on another planet . . .'

The man looked at her gravely. 'This is the same planet. We call you Earth people because you're rooted to what you see as reality. You are earthbound.'

'Earthbound?' Hal didn't think that sounded complimentary.

'It's not better, or worse. Just different. More limited than us, but then you benefit in a lot of material ways.'

'I'm quite happy to be earthbound,' said Hal. 'Only we aren't sure how to get back there, to our earthy place and earthy ways, which suit us very well, it so happens.'

The man raised an eyebrow. 'I'm sure they do,' he said politely. 'There are two ways you can go back to your earthy home. You can walk along that path there until you come to a river. There's a ford there, to go across the river. It's nothing much, just a trickle of water across flat stones. But it's a passing place, and it will take you back to your world.'

Hal's face brightened. 'Thank you,' he said. 'Come on, Gilly. Home!'

'Hang on,' said Gilly. 'There's a catch.'

The tall man smiled. 'Is there?'

'You're right, Gilly,' said Hal. 'What's the other way? You said there were two ways . . .'

'The other way is to find your friend Lugh and to help him in his task, and then, when that part of the pattern is complete, you will find yourselves back in your world again.'

'That's a waste of time. Much better to go back straight now. Via the ford.'

'It could be,' agreed the man.

'Could be?'

'When you cross through the ford, you'll be back in your other world again, but who knows where or when you will find yourselves.'

Hal stared at the man. 'Where or when . . . ? What do you mean?'

'He means,' said Gilly, 'that we could find ourselves in India. A hundred years ago.'

'Or somewhere many years in the future.'

'That's ridiculous,' said Hal, furious. 'It's absurd. What good would that do?'

'Good? How does good come into it?'

'Well, what's the point?' said Gilly. 'Us going back to somewhere we don't belong. What about our own time and where we live?'

'Another sad disappearance of two young people,' the man said. 'It happens a lot, so I understand. People disappearing.'

Gilly stared at him in horror. 'What about our parents?'

'It will cause them great distress, I'm sure,' the man said politely.

'Distress?' said Hal. 'Why are you doing this to us?' His eyes narrowed. 'Anyway, why should we believe you?'

'If we stay with Lugh, and help him, you're saying that we'll get back to where we came from?' Gilly was thinking hard.

'That's right.'

'At the same moment as when we left?'

The man paused briefly. 'Almost the same moment.'

'Don't listen to him,' Hal whispered to Gilly. 'Who is he? Why does he know all this?'

'It ties in with what Lugh said,' Gilly pointed out reasonably.

Hal didn't want reason. 'No,' he said mulishly. 'I'm not convinced. This guy is probably Lugh's uncle or something.'

'We can ask him,' said Gilly.

'Who are you, anyway?' Hal said rudely.

The man bowed. 'I'm the forester. I tend the trees and plants.'

Not much tending, thought Gilly, looking up into the great lattice work of branches above them.

'I guard their magic,' the man explained, a twinkle just visible in his single good eye.

'And all the horrible creatures running up and down in the undergrowth?' Hal was scornful.

'They keep unwelcome visitors away,' the man said mildly.

'How do you know about what Lugh is supposed to do?' said Gilly.

'It's my business to know.'

'He's sent you to persuade us to stay.' Hal was defiant.

'No,' the man said. 'I can't persuade you. All I can do is help you on your way. Backwards or forwards, it's up to you.'

'It isn't a game,' said Gilly.

— 83 —

'No, but it could be a challenge,' said the man. 'If you wanted it to be.'

'If the Vemorians caught us, then we'd have no chance at all of ever getting back to our world.'

Hal couldn't let that pass. 'Not if what he says is true,' he told Gilly. 'If what he says is the way it happens, then we might slip through to our world from anywhere.'

'We don't even know that the Vemorians exist,' went on Gilly. 'It's only what Lugh said. How do we know if anything he says is true?'

The man nodded. 'Of course, you can't. You can't ever know if what anyone says is true. You have to trust the person, and then you believe what they tell you.'

'We don't know Lugh,' said Gilly. 'We've only just met him. How do we know whether we can trust him or not?'

'Knowing's got nothing to do with it,' said Hal, remembering a childhood friend whom he knew extremely well, and who had let him down very badly. 'You can think you know someone really well, and you don't. We might as well trust Lugh as not.'

Gilly sensed that Hal's mood was changing. 'Hal,' she began warningly.

Hal was thinking. 'Do you know where the others are?' he asked abruptly.

'I think I could find them for you,' said the forester.

'Do you know who the head is?'

The man laughed. 'Oh, yes. He's a minor immortal, and he's always up to mischief. He went too far, and that's why he's in trouble now.'

'How does an immortal get into trouble?'

'Offends another immortal who's more powerful than he is.'

— 84 —

'Where are all these immortals?' asked Gilly curiously. 'Apart from the one we've met.'

'They live beyond the Spellbound Gorge, in the Third Lands,' said the man. 'To the east of Vemoria and Tuan.'

'Spellbound Gorge!' said Hal in disbelief.

'One day, your way may take you there,' said the forester. 'In which case, you'll find out just how it got its name.'

'So what's tutti-frutti in the basket doing this side of the gorge, then?'

'The immortals can come across to Vemoria and Tuan whenever they want. Mostly, they're too busy with their own affairs and feuds. But some of the greater gods have an interest in these lands, and they can influence what happens. Indirectly.'

Gilly shook her head. 'This is nonsense. I don't believe any of it. In a moment I'm going to wake up and find myself tucked up in my own bed.'

'Wish you were,' muttered Hal. 'Wish we both were.'

'This isn't a dream,' the forester said. 'There's no escape, no waking up. You have two choices. You go there,' and he pointed to the path which led to the ford, 'and you might find yourself a simple train journey away from home and only a few hours ahead or behind the time you left. Or you could be thousands of miles and centuries away. Which would be quite a different kind of experience. Or,' and he pointed down the darkest, narrowest and most unpleasant path, 'you can accept your challenge, go that way, and take your chance with Lugh and the head.'

He vanished. There was a shimmer of green, a faint spiral of light, and then nothing.

Gilly clutched Hal, who clutched her back.

'This way?'

Gilly nodded, her teethed clamped together to stop them chattering. She shut her eyes, and took a deep breath. 'This way. The dark way,' she added bitterly.

Hal wasn't listening to her. 'Someone's coming.'

'Or something,' said Gilly ominously.

'Lugh!' Hal darted forward as Lugh came running out into the clearing.

'Why didn't you follow me?' said Lugh.

'We met a forester,' said Gilly quickly. 'Have you found them?'

Lugh shook his head. 'No. That donkey must have taken off at a furious pace.'

A thought occurred to Gilly. 'Lugh, is Mab with you?'

'No,' said Lugh. 'I haven't seen her for a while.'

'So where is she?'

'She'll be back,' said Lugh, hoping he sounded more certain than he felt.

'What's that?' said Hal, lifting his head.

'A roar,' said Gilly.

'Sounds like a tiger,' said Hal.

'Tiger?' said Lugh. 'What's a tiger?'

'That,' said Gilly, pointing.

An enormous white tiger stood in the path, its tail lashing. It gave another roar. Then it began to make pouncing movements, but without moving towards them.

Hal clenched his fists, poised himself to run. Then he looked more closely at the huge animal. 'I think it's trying to play!' he said in astonishment.

'Play!' said Gilly, thinking that, whatever it was trying to do, it had an alarmingly hungry look to it.

Lugh stared at the tiger. 'Auntie!' he cried. 'Aunt Mab, it's you, isn't it!'

The tiger dissolved, and Mab stood on the path. 'Of course it's me, you silly boy.'

'Why ever did you have to turn yourself into a tiger and frighten us?' said Gilly crossly. 'As though we weren't frightened enough already.'

Mab gave a sniff. 'I was actually trying to cheer you up. I thought people from where you live were fond of cats. I thought if I became a friendly, purring tabby cat, then it would take your mind off the forest and the lack of head and raven.'

'Tabby?' said Hal.

Mab nodded. 'Yes, tabby. A striped cat. The ones people have as pets. Although I must say, I think it would be a very inconvenient kind of pet.'

'Tabby cats,' pointed out Hal, 'are small, furry creatures. About this size.' He held his hands a cat's length apart. 'What you were was a tiger.'

'A ferocious wild animal that lives in the jungle,' added Gilly.

'Well, I did my best,' said Mab, rather huffily. 'The intention was there, even if the details were slightly wrong.'

A thought had occurred to Lugh. 'Auntie, I thought you couldn't do your spells in the forest.'

'No,' said Mab. 'It's a great nuisance.'

'But you just did one,' said Hal, catching on quickly.

'So I did,' said Mab. 'How surprising.'

'Nothing's different, is it?' Gilly said, looking round. 'Why should Mab's magic suddenly come back?'

'Perhaps it isn't the forest,' said Hal. 'Perhaps it's the head that takes her magic away. Have you ever been in the Wild Forest before, Mab?'

She looked affronted. 'What do you think I am, mad? Of course not. Nobody ever comes in here except by mistake. If we weren't living in such terrible times, I would never have come near this place.'

'So you don't know that it takes away your powers?'

'No,' said Mab. 'But all the witches say it does. There are some dreadful stories about witches in the Wild Forest.'

'Oh, Aunt,' said Lugh. 'Witches' stories! We all know about witches' stories.'

'We do not,' said Mab with dignity.

'Stop arguing,' said Hal. 'The main thing is, Mab has at least some of her powers – that is, until we find the head.'

'You still want to help me?' Lugh gave Hal and Gilly a very shrewd look. 'You didn't follow me.'

'No,' said Gilly. 'We needed to discuss a few things. But we've decided that we're coming with you.'

'You can't manage that evil donk and the head on your own,' said Hal.

'What if we can't find them?' said Lugh.

'Then the Tuans will be in big trouble. That is, if the head is telling the truth.'

'I don't believe a word that head says,' said Gilly. 'He's a liar if ever I heard one.'

Lugh was shocked. He looked round nervously. 'You mustn't say that,' he whispered. 'You mustn't call them names, they don't like it.'

'Nor does anyone,' Hal pointed out.

'OK, let's just say I think he's a truth-twister, who's up to something for his own benefit, not for yours,' said Gilly.

Lugh grinned. 'I expect you're right, but a bargain's a bargain, even with a god-head, and if we can bury him on that hill, he'll have to keep his side of it. Otherwise it'll upset the balance, and he'll be in trouble with all the other demigods.'

'Besides,' said Mab, 'even if we could just escape from this forest, which I would be very glad to do, it wouldn't help you two, would it?'

'Why not?'

'You've accepted a challenge. You won't be able to slip back through to your world until you've completed it, or you're released from it. That's the rule,' said Mab.

Hal and Gilly exchanged glances. It seemed as though the forester knew what he was talking about.

'We know all about that,' said Hal wearily. 'Come on, we haven't got time to stand around and talk. That donkey has probably met up with that wicked giant centipede or whatever it was that attacked me. We'd better get after them.'

'Aunt Mab?' said Lugh.

'A hound, I think,' said Mab, and turned herself with a faint click into an enormous hound, lean, shaggy and very sagacious-looking.

'Good choice,' said Lugh. 'It's a royal Vemorian hunting dog, terrific sense of smell.'

Mab the hound wandered backwards and forwards along the path, its tail waving from side to side. Then it stopped, head on the ground and, making a deep baying sound, set off down the path at great speed.

The others followed, running to keep up with the loping strides of the hound. It came to a fork and unhesitatingly took the left-hand path.

'I bet it's the wrong way,' panted Hal.

'At least that beastly donkey's keeping to the path so far,' said Lugh. 'Anything might happen if it wanders off into the trees.'

The hound went on, nose still down. 'They've come a long way,' said Lugh.

'Donkey probably bolted,' said Hal.

— 89 —

'That would make the head sea-sick,' said Gilly. 'I wish Mab would slow down, I'm getting a stitch. Oh!'

Gilly came to an abrupt halt as did the others. The hound had led them into another clearing. There was the donkey, its flanks heaving. The raven had hopped on to a nearby branch. The head, it was clear, was in a most ungodly temper.

'If you don't get us out of this forest NOW,' it boomed at Lugh, 'it's going to be very much the worse for you and your useless friends.'

'Useless! Useless!' echoed the raven breathlessly. 'He means it, you know, he means it.'

'Mab?' said Lugh hopefully.

The hound bounced towards him, slobbering and sending flecks of saliva over the head.

'Help,' said Gilly. 'That's not going to improve his temper.'

'Quick,' said Hal. 'She's off.'

'We've found the donkey,' said Gilly, as the party lurched into movement. 'What's she after now?'

'Don't know,' said Hal. 'It's better than staying here and being ripped up by that head.'

'True,' said Gilly, breaking into a run.

Lugh, the donkey's halter held firmly in one hand with the rope twisted round his wrist to stop any further escapes, brought up the rear. The raven flew from branch to branch, cawing loudly and unnecessarily.

'Water,' cried Hal, as they juddered to a halt.

'This isn't the ford, is it?' said Gilly uneasily.

'He said that was a trickle,' Hal reminded her. 'And it was in the opposite direction.'

'I don't think that means anything in this forest,' said Gilly.

Mab was running up and down on the bank of what was a wide and swiftly-flowing river. Then, with a series of important-sounding barks, she bounded out of sight behind a tree. A few seconds later, Lugh and Hal saw her, back in her normal form, beckoning to them.

'Mustn't let the head see me,' she whispered as they drew near. 'Must keep well out of sight. And range. Or my magic will go again; one look from him, nasty old thing, and I'll be no good again.'

'How do we get across the river?'

'Good heavens, don't ask me,' said Mab. 'It's the boundary of the forest, I can tell you that, but I haven't the slightest idea how you can get across it. That's your problem, I'm not here to solve problems.'

She was gone. Hal and Lugh looked at each other. Hal shrugged his shoulders.

'So,' said the head. 'This is the edge of the forest. Luckily for you,' he added grimly. 'Now, take us across.'

The three of them looked across the black water to the shore on the other side.

'And just how do we do that?' said Gilly.

Eleven

*F*OR THE FIRST TIME, HAL WISHED HE HAD PAID more attention to survival programmes on TV, where teams lashed together oil drums and old tyres to get themselves across a river.

'It wouldn't help,' said Gilly practically. 'There's nothing like that here to make a raft.'

'Cut a tree down? Float it across?' suggested Hal rather hopelessly.

Gilly looked at him in despair. 'Come on, Hal,' she said. 'How do we chop one of these monsters down, to start with? We haven't got an axe, and even if we had, it would take days.'

'Yes, and it would fall on us and squash us all flat, knowing our luck,' agreed Hal.

'I don't think the forest would like you attacking a tree,' said Lugh.

They looked round at the great wall of huge, strange trees and densely-growing plants. Great pods of seeds dropped from flowers blooming far, far above them. They fell with a soft splat into the water, and floated slowly away.

'OK,' said Hal. 'Not one of my better ideas.'

'Let's think,' said Gilly. 'How can you cross a river?'

'Over a bridge,' said Lugh. 'But there isn't one. Not here, in any case, and we can't walk along the bank;

except at this spot, the trees grow almost into the water.'

'You can float across on something,' said Hal. 'Only there's nothing for us to float on.'

'Or you can wade across,' said Gilly.

'Don't be ridiculous,' said Hal irritably. 'It's far too deep.'

'How do you know?' said Gilly.

Hal peered into the water. 'You can't see the bottom.'

'That's because it's overshadowed by these trees. But look, further out, where it gets lighter, you can see some weed drifting.'

'So?'

'So, it might be a lot shallower than it looks.'

Lugh got down on his hands and knees and gingerly put his arm into the water. 'Hey,' he said, springing up. 'I can feel the bottom.'

'This is the edge,' said Hal sceptically. 'It probably falls away really steeply once you get out from the bank. We'd be swept away; look how fast the water's moving.'

'I think we should try it,' said Lugh.

'We may as well,' said Gilly. 'If someone goes in first, and we all hold on to them, then they won't be swept away.'

While he had been investigating the river, Lugh had slackened his hold on the donkey's halter. Now it jerked its head up, yanking itself free, and with a purposeful look on its face it slithered down the little slope into the river.

Hal, Lugh and Gilly watched, transfixed, as it moved neatly forward, paying no attention to the stream of commands and abuse issuing out of the basket from the head. The water barely covered its fetlocks.

'Ah,' said Hal.

'We'd better get after it,' said Lugh, bending down to take off his sandals.

'Bags I not last,' said Gilly. 'There might be crocodiles.'

There weren't. The whole party tripped sedately and effortlessly across the broad strip of water and clambered easily up the other side.

'Well,' said Hal, looking back across the water. 'I say, who's that? Is it Mab?'

It was. She was flitting up and down on the opposite shore, apparently wringing her hands.

'Just come across,' Gilly shouted. 'It's easy!'

'I can't,' came the sad cry from the other side.

Lugh gave an exclamation. 'Of course, she can't! Witches can't cross running water.'

'You can't be serious,' said Hal.

'It's true,' said Lugh. 'I'll have to go back and bring her across.'

'Leave her,' cried the head imperiously. 'We don't need her, or want her.'

'No,' said the raven, who had flown across to join them. 'We don't want her, we don't want her.'

'Too bad,' said Hal, taking his shoes off again. 'We can't leave her in the Wild Forest, goodness knows what might happen to her.'

He waded back into the river and splashed back to the other side. 'Come on,' he said to Mab. 'You won't fall. You ride on my back, and hold on tight, and you'll be OK.'

Mab dithered. 'It isn't safe,' she cried.

A scream rang across the water.

'Hal!'

It was Gilly. 'Hal,' she screamed again. 'Quick, oh, quick! Look at the water.'

Hal took one look, and stood rigid with horror.

The calm river was no longer a placid stream. There were ominous ripples running across the surface of the water.

Hal stood in the shallows, gazing at what seemed to be a great cloud rolling towards him.

It wasn't a cloud.

'Hal,' screamed Gilly, her voice magnified by panic. 'It's a WAVE.'

It was. Hal's eyes focused properly and he blinked unbelievingly at the huge wave, a wall of water as high as a house which was moving inexorably in his direction.

Mab, all arguments forgotten, hurled herself on to Hal's back. He plunged back into the dark water and tore across, with great lunging strides. He could hear the roar of the approaching wave as he reached the other side, and with a last, desperate effort, he threw himself on the shore. Mab rolled off and ran instantly up to join the others; Gilly grabbed Hal by the hand to help pull him out of reach of the implacable, boiling wall of water that was foaming towards him. With a strength he didn't know he had, he leapt, scrabbling for a footing, and somehow hauled himself further up.

Lugh had dragged the donkey up from the shore and pushed it on to higher ground. Now he leant down, and together with Gilly, heaved Hal up the last few yards to safety. They stood, panting and terrified, as the river crashed and pounded below them. The banks that they had just before been standing on had vanished on both sides of the river, and there was turbulent, black and malevolent water as far as the eye could see.

'Well,' said Mab, brushing the water off herself. 'I don't think I'll try going back across there in a hurry. Whatever happened?'

'Whatever it was, it happened very quickly,' said Lugh. 'At a guess, I would say that someone – or something – knows we're on our way.'

'It doesn't take a great brain to work that one out,' said the head sarcastically. 'I don't suppose you have any idea how uncomfortable all this has been for me, lurching around in this basket?'

'It's not exactly a holiday of a lifetime for any of us,' said Hal, his temper rising.

'Hal,' said Gilly. 'Calm down. At least we're out of that dreadful wood, and we're all safe.'

Safe they might be, for the moment, but they had other problems. Food, for one. Water, for another. And shelter for the coming night. Lugh was worried.

'We'd better eat while we can,' he said, opening one of the saddlebags and moving away to be at a distance from the head. The head was either asleep or sulking. The raven sat on the donkey's withers, watching the others with a cold round eye. The donkey tugged gratefully at the thick grass.

Lugh pulled out some bread, the last of what he had packed so many hours before in the village. 'There's some fruit, too.'

'Are these apricots?' said Gilly, inspecting a small pink fruit.

'I've never seen a bright pink apricot,' said Hal. 'Tastes like one, though.' Pink juice dripped down his chin. 'Pretty good. What are these, Lugh?'

Lugh's mind was on other matters. 'What? Oh, we call them *casash*. They grow everywhere. People make them into jam.'

'What's the matter, Lugh?' asked Gilly, her mouth full of *casash*.

'We have to find somewhere to sleep tonight,' said Lugh.

Hal looked around him. After their frantic escape from the troublesome black river, they had climbed up a steep path and found themselves in a wide meadow of thick grass. 'It's so mild, can't we sleep in the open?'

'No,' said Lugh. 'It wouldn't be safe.'

'Not safe?' said Gilly, dismayed. The darkness and panic and danger of the forest and river seemed a long way away; this was a different world.

'Yes, it is quite different,' said Lugh. 'It's Vemoria. You can tell because of the neat hedging and the well-kept trees. Soon we'll come across some ditches and canals, we're bound to.'

'Canals?' Hal was interested.

'Yes, the Vemorians use water for everything; I told you they were water-mad. They don't have roads, they have canals or use rivers. They're very organized.'

'So why isn't it safe for us to sleep out here?'

'It isn't allowed,' said Lugh. 'By law, you have to register if you aren't spending a night in your own home. It doesn't matter if you're staying with a friend or in an inn, you have to fill in a form just the same. The Wardens come round every week, or twice a week, I forget which. Checking.'

'Like they do in some countries abroad,' said Gilly. 'You know, Hal, all those registration forms with passport numbers and so on that you have to fill in. The police take them.'

'Private houses?' said Hal. 'Guests? Friends staying overnight?'

'Yes,' said Lugh.

'Surely nobody bothers,' said Hal.

'They do,' said Lugh. 'It would never happen in Tuan, we just aren't like that. But they're very officious, the Vemorians. If anyone didn't fill in the forms and give them to the Wardens, then the neighbours would find out. They'd waste no time letting the Wardens know about it.'

'That's ghastly!' burst out Gilly.

'Bureaucratic,' said Hal. 'So we have to stay in an inn where we can fill in all the forms.'

'Only we can't,' said Lugh, looking worried again. 'I can, because I've got identity papers.'

'You're a Tuan,' Gilly pointed out.

'Yes, but most of us have Vemorian papers for when we need them. Just in case. When we come over on business, or to see friends . . .'

'Well, where did you get them?'

'There was someone in the village who did them.'

'So what do we do?' said Hal. 'We can't go to an inn, because we don't have any papers. We'll have to camp out, illegal or not, and just hope that no one spots us.'

Lugh shook his head. 'We can't risk it. They have dogs, very highly trained. And having the head with us . . . It wouldn't be safe.'

'That's no good, then,' said Gilly. 'But we can't stay at an inn anyway, Hal. We don't have any money.'

'Money's not a problem,' said Lugh quickly. 'Don't forget, I've brought a lot of money with us, the money my uncle left behind for me.'

'Can we buy papers?' asked Gilly. 'Surely some people aren't afraid of the Wardens?'

'All the Vemorians are,' said Lugh. 'But you're right. In any of the bigger towns there are people from other countries, and if you've got the right contacts, you can get anything. Our problem is time. We've only got about three hours, by my reckoning, until curfew.'

'Curfew?'

'Yes, there's a curfew in Vemoria. A late one in the capital, but out here on the borders it'll be quite early.'

'Do you know where we are?' asked Hal. 'Is there a town near here?'

'That's part of the problem,' said Lugh. 'I think I know roughly where we are, but that's not much use.'

The donkey, still grazing, suddenly looked up. Its ears, which had flopped down on either side, flicked up and forward. It let out a loud bray, which sounded exactly like a creaking gate.

'It's spotted something,' said Lugh.

'That,' said Gilly, pointing to a path beyond the edge of the meadow. There was an answering bray, and two ears and another donkey head appeared over the hedge.

'Strange-looking donkey,' said Hal. 'Look at that big stripe down its nose.'

Lugh's eyes narrowed. 'I know that donkey. There can't be another one like it . . . It must be . . . YES!'

He started to leap up and down, waving his arms and shouting. Gilly and Hal looked at each other; the raven, woken from its black and brooding nap, fluttered into the air with a disapproving caw. 'What a noise, what a noise!'

Lugh was running across the meadow now, heading for the hedge. The donkey galloped along beside him, with loud shouts of rage and fury coming from the head, which was having another rough ride in its basket. The donkey got to the hedge first, and skidded to a halt, before thrusting its head over the hedge to bump noses with the other donkey.

Hal and Gilly followed, not at quite the same speed.

'Lugh can certainly run,' grumbled Hal, never one to exert himself necessarily.

Lugh turned round, a wide smile on his face. 'Hal, Gilly, this is Jouri.'

Hal and Gilly found themselves being looked over by a slight, merry little man, with a deeply-tanned face and a pair of grey eyes which looked startlingly light and penetrating.

'Earth people,' he said at once. 'Now, that is interesting. When was the last time we had visitors from there, Lugh?'

Lugh thought for a moment. 'Not so very long ago, surely.'

'When there was all that trouble.'

Lugh cast a swift glance at the basket, and shook his head slightly at Jouri. He mouthed some words at him; Jouri's eyes opened wide, and he whistled in surprise.

The head spoke. 'What's going on?' it said. 'Take this lid off, I feel extremely uncomfortable, and judging by the accent, you haven't met up with a Vemorian.'

'We have to be careful,' Lugh explained to Jouri, as he pulled the top of the basket and took the cover off the head.

Jouri stepped back a pace or two. 'Wow,' he said. 'That's a bit of a responsibility. Whatever are you doing with it, and here in Vemoria of all places?'

'There's a lot to explain,' said Lugh.

'Great,' said Jouri. 'I love a good story. Where are you staying?'

'That's a problem,' said Lugh. 'These two haven't got any papers.'

'They'll need them,' said Jouri instantly. 'Can't tell you how tight things are, especially here, near the border.'

'I can guess,' said Lugh.

The head was getting impatient. 'Time to move on,' it commanded. 'We have a long journey, and we have already wasted too much time.'

'We're doing our best,' protested Hal.

'Silence, silence,' said the raven.

'You're travelling on your own legs,' said the head rather petulantly. 'If you were in my state, you'd resent every hour.'

Gilly felt he had a point, but Hal had little sympathy for the head. 'Tough,' he said brutally. 'We can't just go careering across the countryside; I don't know anything about this country, but anyone can tell it's a place where you have to do everything by the book. Otherwise you'll stand out like a sore thumb.'

Jouri nodded in agreement. 'And with the way the Vemorians are about heads . . . well, sir, if they once clapped eyes on you, you'd have no chance of meeting up with the rest of you, wherever it is. No chance at all.'

The head made a grumbling noise, and glared at Lugh.

'Can you help us, Jouri?' said Lugh, looking directly at his friend.

Jouri drew in his breath. 'It's dangerous,' he said. 'Dangerous and tricky. But I suspect you wouldn't be over here if it wasn't something important, and I'm sure these two wouldn't have come across without a reason . . .'

'I called them,' Lugh confessed. 'I needed help.'

'You can call; anyone can call, but how often do they come?' said Jouri wisely. 'No, no, there's a purpose to their coming, you'll see. And why are there two others, who must have come through at the same time?'

—— 101 ——

'Others?' said Hal warily. 'What others?'

'Other youngsters,' said Jouri. 'From your world, it sounds like. Friends of yours?'

Hal and Gilly looked at each other.

'Bram,' said Hal.

'And Erica,' said Gilly.

'What joy,' said Hal unenthusiastically.

'Girl and boy?' asked Jouri. 'That'll be them. Boy's working down on the canals. The girl . . . funny thing, that. She doesn't seem to be working for anyone. Living more as a member of the family, so I hear. At the house of . . . Well, never mind that.'

'Is Bram a slave?' Much as Gilly disliked her cousin, she didn't like the thought of that at all.

'He's quite all right,' said Jouri. 'Nothing you can do about it if he isn't. As it happens, he's not too badly off. Now, papers, papers . . .' He wound a thick curl of his shiny brown hair round a long lean finger as he thought. 'No one will take these two for Vemorians,' he said finally. 'They look all wrong. They'll have to be from beyond the Gonelands.'

'Isn't Vemoria at war with them?' said Lugh, sounding surprised.

'Not at the moment,' replied Jouri. 'Treaty, while they concentrate on rolling up the Tuans. There are a lot of Gonelanders about just now, no one will think it strange.'

'All very well,' said Hal, who wasn't too sure he wanted to be a Gonelander; goodness knows what kind of people they were. 'How do we get hold of these papers? Mug a couple of them and nick their documents?'

Jouri looked shocked. 'I wouldn't advise that at all, it would be very foolish. No one mugs anyone in

— 102 —

Vemoria and gets away with it. No, no, we need to go and look up Venturia. You remember her, Lugh?'

'Is she living here?'

Jouri nodded. 'Got a good business, transcribing documents, you know how good she is at that kind of thing, Deals in maps, too; the Vemorians think a lot of her.'

'Who's Venturia?' Gilly asked.

'A distant cousin,' said Lugh. 'I didn't know she was over here, I thought she would have fled with all the others.'

'Not her,' said Jouri. 'Business comes first, and of course, she's able to help Tuans in all kinds of ways. The Vemorians keep an eye on her, but she's very clever, too clever for them.'

'How far away is she?'

Jouri thought for a moment. 'Take you about an hour,' he said. 'Less if you went by water, but that's out of the question if you haven't got papers. We'll have to slip into the town without being seen. If she's there, she'll be able to fix you up.'

'Let's go.'

Twelve

*L*UGH CLAMPED THE LID DOWN ON THE BASKET, and clipped the saddlebag back in place. Ignoring the imperious voice thundering from the basket, he swung the donkey round and headed for the gate to the meadow.

'Is this taking you out of your way?' Hal asked Jouri. He was curious about who he was and why he was in Vemoria.

'No, I can go this way,' said Jouri. The donkeys walked side by side, their tails swishing together. Lugh and Jouri at their heads talked in soft voices. Hal glowered at them.

'You look just like the head,' said Gilly thoughtlessly.

'Oh, shut up,' said Hal. 'I hate being at everyone's beck and call. It's supposed to be a challenge for us, and all we get to do is be bossed around by whoever's about.'

'We're strangers. We know nothing.'

'We might know more than they think, only nobody's asking.'

Lugh turned round for a moment. 'Don't fall behind,' he called to them. 'We need to get to Venturia's well before curfew. Jouri says that's about an hour after sundown, and the sun is already low on the horizon.'

'There's another funny thing,' said Gilly, hoping to distract Hal. Stubborn was bad enough; moody was hell. And Hal's moods could last for days. 'It seems to be well into autumn here, look at the leaves. Yet it was early autumn in Tuan, I'm sure it was.'

'And high summer back in England,' said Hal.

'We weren't actually in the forest for very long.'

'Seemed like an age,' said Hal grumpily.

'Obviously, it was full of magic.'

'Magic,' said Hal, about to add 'and who over the age of five believes in magic'; then he caught sight of the basket and the raven, and decided not to say anything more.

The raven flapped importantly over to them. 'Hurry up, don't dawdle, don't dawdle,' she said irritatingly.

'Talking ravens,' said Hal. 'This is a farce.'

Gilly thought of the huge and powerful head sitting incongruously in the basket, and wished it were. 'And I don't like the sound of the Vemorians. I bet they go in for taxes.'

'Police state,' said Hal, forgetting he was in a mood, and becoming interested. 'Telephone-tapping . . . Only there aren't any telephones. Spies, intrigues. Messengers. Secrets. Plots . . .'

This might appeal to Hal, who loved reading books about spies and grim societies. It held no joy for Gilly. Police states tend not to be very keen on artists or anyone who was in the least bit different. That was the extent of her knowledge about them, and it wasn't encouraging.

The path, which had been soft, with white sand and grass growing through in patches, began to look more tended. Its edges were more precise, with the inevitable hedges neatly cut on either side. There were symmetrically-laid stones now, in what would otherwise be cart ruts. They passed a group of stone houses. They were in excellent condition, with everything squared off and in perfect order. Their occupants came to the doors and watched silently and suspiciously as the two donkeys and the accompanying people went past.

'Don't smile,' hissed Jouri. 'Smiling makes them suspicious.'

'Don't they smile?' whispered Gilly.

'Yes, but never at strangers.'

'They must make a lot of enemies.'

'They don't have to make enemies, mostly they reckon anyone they don't know is an enemy. All foreigners are enemies, that goes without saying.'

'How depressing. How do foreigners survive?'

'They need them, and they know they do. That's being reasonable. But they still hate them. They only feel safe with foreigners when they're slaves.'

'Slaves.' The word brought home to Hal and Gilly just how far they were from home. 'Like being back in Ancient Greece,' said Gilly.

'Worse,' said Hal. 'There were compensations to Ancient Greece. I don't think there are any compensations here.'

'Except that we aren't slaves,' said Gilly.

'Not yet,' said Hal.

'And Bram and Erica are.'

'Why do they need foreigners?' asked Hal, wanting to divert Gilly's attention away from Bram and Erica.

'Trade,' said Jouri. 'Skills that they don't possess; special crafts, all kinds of luxuries that they'd like to do without but are too fond of. They don't cook very well, for example, and the climate doesn't allow them to grow all kinds of crops which they need or want.' His face grew wary. 'Now, no more talking, please. We're coming to a village. We need to get through without being stopped.'

'Where do you think Mab is?' Hal whispered into Gilly's ear.

'Goodness knows,' said Gilly. 'I can't see Vemoria being her cup of tea.'

Hal slid past the donkeys and spoke quietly to Jouri. 'Why are all the houses looking the other way? This is the main street, isn't it?'

Jouri spoke almost without moving his lips. 'Yes, but roads aren't important. All the houses look out over the canal, it runs parallel to this. That's the main thoroughfare, they go everywhere by water.'

'Oh, yes; Lugh told us.'

'Quiet, now. We don't want to attract attention.'

'They'll hear the donkeys.'

'And they'll look, but they'll just see foreign traders, too insignificant to go by water. It's time for their evening meal, we should be all right.'

Gilly felt distinctly uneasy as they walked silently past the row of neat houses. Lights flickered out from one or two windows, but mostly the windows were dark. She supposed that they would have their main living rooms at the front, looking over the water.

They left the village behind them without any mishaps, to Jouri's evident relief.

'We get off this path now,' he said, striding forward. He suddenly ducked down beside the hedge, and disappeared. They all stared. Then his head bobbed up on the other side. 'There's a gap,' he said. 'You can't see it unless you know it's there. Lugh, bring the donkeys through.'

The donkeys weren't at all keen. Ears went back, hard little hooves dug into the sandy soil at the side of the road, tails twitched.

Jouri darted back through the hedge, a springy twig in his hand. His own donkey took one look and scrambled through. Lugh's donkey stood firmly where it was.

'Hold on,' said Hal. 'I don't think it can get through the hedge with the panniers on. We'll have to take at least the basket off, and pass it through.'

The raven, who had travelled along in contemptuous silence, hopped over the hedge and looked threateningly at Hal.

'Be careful, be careful. You carry a god, remember that. Yes, remember that.'

'Oh, go away,' said Hal, crossly. 'Your head's just got to put up with it. When you're a disembodied head, you don't have much say in the matter.'

Gilly unthreaded the basket, and with Hal's help lowered it to the ground. They could see the baleful, glowing eyes looking out at them. 'Peasants,' the head hissed at them. 'Serfs. Scum of the earth.'

Hal stood where he was, and folded his arms. 'You call us names, and we leave you where you are.'

'I have power,' the head began.

'Not like you did before,' said Hal. He turned to look at Gilly, surprise written all over his face. 'It's true, you know. He can't make me do things the way he did when we started.'

'It's because you've come of your own free will,' said a familiar voice. Mab materialized beside them.

'Mab, where have you been?' said Gilly, strangely pleased to see her.

'Out of sight, out of mind,' said Mab vaguely. 'I don't like Vemoria, and I can tell you for nothing, the Vemorians simply HATE witches.'

Thirteen

IT WAS A WALLED TOWN. THE DEFENCES WERE NO longer needed, Jouri explained in a whisper as they slid along in the shadows cast by the wall; they were a relic from a long time ago. Each town then had been ruled by its own lord, and naturally, every town was at war with every other one. This was before the Twelve had taken over, bringing a lot of law and even more order to the previously unruly Vemorians.

'The Twelve?' asked Gilly when Jouri explained this to them. It had an ominous ring to it.

'Twelve families who rule Vemoria,' said Jouri. 'Quiet, now.'

They had come to a door set into the thick stone. It was a big door, clearly very old, studded with some dark metal. Jouri looked round quickly to make sure they were alone, and then gave the door a light push. It swung open, easily and silently. Jouri saw Hal's astonished face.

'Things aren't always what they seem,' he said in a low voice. 'Because the door looks impregnable, because it leads out to a road and not on to a waterway, they never check it. We Tuans are very good at doors, and we've done some work on this one; we keep it oiled and opening smoothly . . . Very convenient.'

He threaded his way through narrow streets. The ground was slightly sandy, and the donkeys' hooves made no sound. 'These are warehouses,' Jouri whispered. 'No one comes to this quarter at night, except later, when the watchmen make their rounds.'

'Thieves?' asked Gilly.

Jouri shook his head. 'Too risky. The owners leave their slaves to sleep in there. They'd raise the alarm.'

Gilly stared up at the dark buildings, with tiny, shuttered windows set high up under the eaves, and shuddered. Lugh, too, looked up, wondering if any of his numerous family were perhaps locked up there, swept away by the Vemorians on one of their raids.

'Unlikely,' said Jouri. 'Your family would be too valuable. They'd make them into house slaves.'

Lugh didn't find that a specially comforting thought. Mab didn't either. A lot of Lugh's family on her side were of a witchy persuasion, and they'd get no welcome at all from any Vemorian.

The ground changed from its sandy surface to thick cobbles. The sun was sinking into the western clouds, and long shadows fell across their way. Twinkles of light appeared in some of the houses; they were away from the warehouses now, and, said Jouri, in more danger. 'Not too fast,' he said. 'That would attract suspicion. Just walk normally, talk a little, look serious, as though we've all been out on business. The Vemorians respect business and business people.'

Gilly immediately felt like an orang-utan. Business-like! How could she or Hal look businesslike?

'You can't,' said Lugh, with a sudden laugh. 'But you can at least try to look as though you've been out with your elders and betters, learning the business!'

Jouri gave another quick look round, and then slipped between two houses. In the shadows, they hadn't even noticed the entrance to the alleyway. He went rapidly past the first five doors, and then tapped quietly on the sixth. Two long knocks, a quick tap, a pause, then two more longer knocks.

Silence. In the distance, voices rose as a group of citizens parted for the night, making their way back to their various homes in the short time left before curfew.

The door opened, quite suddenly. A tall, dark, frowning woman stood there, not at all welcoming. Gilly felt as though there was a stone lodged at the bottom of her stomach. Then the woman caught sight of Jouri, and smiled. The smile became a wide gesture of welcome and delight as Mab came out of the shadows. The woman made a sign for them to come in, and they crossed the threshold, donkeys and all. The door shut noiselessly behind them.

They weren't inside the house but in another passageway. Jouri led the donkeys past another door and out into a courtyard.

'No lights,' said Venturia, swinging open a stable door. 'Room for them both in here. You know where the hay is, Jouri.'

Her eyes narrowed as they took in the raven and the basket. 'I know you,' she said to the raven. 'I never thought the day would come when you were under my roof. And what's that in the basket?' She reached over and plucked the lid off. The great head, seeming almost to glow in the half light, glared balefully out.

'Ha, it's you, is it?' she said. 'Been up to mischief again, have you?'

The raven, her feathers ruffled and then smoothed again, squawked at her. 'Disrespectful woman. This is one of the Immortals, a demigod.'

'What goings-on, then, for a demigod!' she said

scornfully. 'Well, I suppose I can't leave you out here all night; you'd frighten the donkeys. Inside with you, but not a word when the Wardens come round.'

'Wardens?' said Jouri, alarmed.

'Yes, Wardens,' said Venturia. 'You can be sure that someone in the street will have seen you arrive. I suppose these three haven't got papers, eh?'

'I have,' said Lugh. 'These two come from another country. They were called.'

'Came through, did they?' Venturia looked at Hal and Gilly with a trace of respect in her face. 'I'll do papers for them saying they're from the Gonelands. There are a quite a few from there in the big cities, so I hear, but no one in this part of the world will know what they're like.'

She picked up the head effortlessly; she was strong as well as tall. Then she ushered them out of the yard and through another old wooden door and inside the house.

'Will the papers take long?' said Lugh.

She shook her head. 'I keep some ready, only the details to fill in.'

'What would happen if someone found out you forged papers?' asked Hal indiscreetly.

'Never ask,' she said. 'The penalties are not what you want to be thinking about at your age. Put you clean off your supper.'

Gilly didn't like the sound of that, but she did like the sound of supper. 'Can we help? With anything?'

'I'll cook,' said Jouri, who was obviously quite at home in the house. 'But first, we'd better get these two stowed away where any visitors won't notice them.'

'Stow me away at your peril, at your peril!' said the raven. 'I am a sacred bird!'

'And much good that will do you among the

— 113 —

Vemorians,' said Jouri. 'Come on, now, upstairs with you both, and if you're a good bird, I'll bring you up a nice bit of steak.'

The big black bird hopped crossly up the stairs, one step at a time, cawing to Jouri to be careful with the head. 'This is no way to treat a god. What a shame, what a shame, what a shame!'

Jouri came down with a broad grin on his face. 'That's me cursed to the Spellbound Gorge and beyond,' he said.

'What have you done with the head?' asked Hal.

'Stowed it away in one of the rooms upstairs. I put some dirty linen on top of him, just in case any nosy warden takes a look.'

'Good,' said Hal. 'Serve him right.'

'You sit yourself down,' said Jouri. 'You've had a hard journey. I'll see to the food, and then, when all the papers are in order, we can eat, and you can tell me and Venturia just what is going on.'

'The tale of the head,' said Hal, plonking himself down in a carved wooden chair.

Gilly sank into a long seat with a low back which was piled high with fat, brocaded cushions. 'Jouri's right,' she said. 'It's been a long day.'

'Mmm,' said Lugh, relaxing into a pile of cushions of his own. 'And we've come a long way.'

'Into the lion's den, you would say where you come from,' said Mab cheerfully, putting her head round the door.

'That's not very encouraging,' said Gilly.

'No, but she's right,' pointed out Hal.

'What is it, Auntie?' asked Lugh, his eyes drooping.

'Just checking how tall these two are . . . stand up a

moment, Hal. Half a head taller than Lugh, and Gilly the same as Lugh. Venturia needs to hurry, I feel trouble coming.'

The three of them were feeling too sleepy and hungry to pay much attention to what Mab had said.

'Always rabbiting on,' said Lugh, his eyes now closed.

'How very peaceful it all is,' said Gilly with a huge yawn.

Hal said nothing at all. He was falling asleep. He would have fallen asleep.

Then the Wardens came.

Fourteen

*B*ANG. BANG. BANG.
Three peremptory knocks.

Venturia went to the big old door and pulled back the heavy bolts. She stood blocking the doorway.

'Well?' she demanded.

There were two Wardens. As Venturia opened the door, they took a pace forward, intending to come into the house. Then, since Venturia didn't move, they had to stop, their faces about an inch away from her. One was very tall and rather thin; his companion was short and stocky.

'We are the Wardens of the Night,' said the tall one impassively. 'We have right of entry.'

Venturia let them in. 'Of course,' she said, smiling a tight smile that came nowhere near her eyes. 'You want to see my guest records.'

The tall one came in and strode towards the hearth, his dark eyes flickering round the room. Short and stocky went to stand beside him.

'Visitors were reported here this evening. Just before curfew.'

The tall one had an unpleasant, gravelly voice. He spoke very fast.

'I wonder who told you that,' said Venturia.

'Weren't you going to report the visitors?' said the stocky one, his voice rich with suspicion.

'I always report my visitors,' said Venturia. 'My neighbours need not be so vigilant.'

'Vigilance keeps the State safe,' said the tall one.

'They should keep their eyes open for more serious offenders,' said Venturia.

'Do you know of any such?' said the stocky one in an eager voice.

The tall one frowned. 'If she knows of any offenders or lawbreakers and hasn't already reported them, then she's in serious trouble.'

'I don't,' said Venturia. 'But I think some of my neighbours do.'

'Make a note,' instructed the tall one.

The short, stocky man pulled out a pad and made a few squiggles on it. Hal, watching silently from his seat, thought that he looked for all the world like a small bull, with his flushed face and tight, curly red hair.

The stocky one's attention was diverted towards Mab, now lying stretched out regally, her fronded tail thumping slightly.

His eyes narrowed as much as they could, being, as they were, small and piggy. 'That's a Royal Hunting Hound,' he said with authority. 'Have you a licence for such an animal? Ordinary citizens are not permitted to keep these hounds.'

Crash!

Venturia knocked a plate off the long, low table which ran along one wall. It broke into several pieces, startling everyone.

'It's nothing,' said Venturia, picking up the remains. 'It can be repaired.'

'Was it valuable?' asked tall and thin. 'An antique? Had you registered it as part of the State heritage?'

'It was just an ordinary plate,' said Venturia. 'I ate an apple earlier this evening and left the plate here.'

The Wardens looked even more disapproving. Leaving plates about was slovenly. And why had she brought the plate in there in the first place? Plates and food should stay in the kitchen and dining room. Plates in strange places indicated more slovenliness. Then to break the plate . . . Good Vemorians were orderly in everything they did. Carrying plates about the place and breaking them was not orderly.

They turned their attention back to the dog, who in some strange way didn't look such a noble hound. Her ears were slightly longer, her coat rougher, her tail more straggly and, although she was still a large and intelligent-looking dog, she now looked much more ordinary than she had before.

The tall Warden shook his head. 'That's no Royal Hunting Hound,' he said in a definite voice. 'Same sort of size, but obviously not a pure-bred anything.'

As the stocky Warden looked hard at Mab, a puzzled expression on his face, Jouri edged over to Hal and breathed into his ear. 'There's more to this than it seems. These aren't ordinary Wardens, they're Zed Wardens. High-ups.'

This meant nothing to Hal, but the slight movement had caught the tall Warden's attention. He held out a hand. 'Papers,' he said curtly.

Hal said nothing, but he and Gilly looked nervously at Venturia.

'I have their papers,' she said smoothly. 'Naturally, they handed them to me as soon as they arrived. They know the rules.'

The Wardens flipped through the papers, reading details, and then flicking his eyes over the visitors. He handed Lugh and Jouri's papers back very quickly, but was much more interested in Hal and Gilly's.

'From the Gonelands,' he said slowly. 'Under age. Travelling alone? That is forbidden.'

Jouri made a throat-clearing noise. 'Um, they're with me.'

'Why are they with you?'

Good question, thought Gilly. She had a horrible feeling that they weren't going to slide out of this very easily.

'I've worked with their father for many years. He wants them to see Vemoria. A country for which he has great admiration.'

Gilly thought it very funny that Jouri sounded so unlike his normal self now that he was talking to the Wardens, but she was impressed by his swift and easy lies.

The Warden looked at her and Hal. 'What does your father do?' he asked, striking them both dumb.

'Precision metalwork,' said Jouri swiftly. 'Very specialized. I trade in such things, as you see from my papers. He makes a pipe-connector which is in use all over Vemoria.'

The Wardens grew more respectful. 'To do with water, then?'

'Oh, yes,' said Jouri. 'That's why he has so much respect for Vemoria and wants his children to become familiar with our ways.'

The tall Warden began to look more human, but Hal, glancing at the stocky one's face, thought that he didn't look particularly convinced.

Venturia thought it was time to be rid of the Wardens before they asked just one too many nosy questions. They would be bound to hit on one that she or Jouri couldn't fudge an answer to.

'If the papers are in order—' she began.

The shorter Warden glared at her. He knew something was wrong, he was certain that all was not as it seemed here. 'We'll just have a look round,' he said.

'Can they?' Hal whispered to Jouri. 'Don't they need special permission?'

Jouri pulled a face. 'Not them! This is Vemoria; if you wear a uniform, you can do what you like, and no sensible citizen ever challenges a Warden.'

They could hear the Wardens clumping their way up the stairs. Gilly found herself digging her nails into the palms of her hands. What if they looked in the linen basket? Found the head? Or even went near it – would the head have the sense to keep his big, arrogant mouth shut? She doubted it.

The Wardens clattered back downstairs, investigated the kitchen and the other downstairs rooms. The door banged as they went out into the yard.

Hal exchanged glances with Gilly. No one in the parlour said a word. Clatter, clang. The Wardens were back. They were frowning. Disappointed because they haven't found anything, thought Venturia.

'Two donkeys,' said the stocky Warden. He addressed Jouri. 'Are they both yours?'

'Because,' added the tall Warden, 'you,' and he glared at Venturia, 'don't have a permit for a donkey.'

The stocky one didn't look too pleased at his colleague's interruption.

'Both mine,' said Jouri quickly.

'Why do you need two donkeys for your samples, which are all very small?'

Jouri wasn't fazed at all. 'I take back other samples from Vemoria. Our State is encouraging us to sell to the Gonelands, as of course you know.'

It was perfectly true, and it was clear that the

Wardens, although not entirely trusting Jouri, could hardly argue with him about that.

'They're very specialized,' Jouri explained, as Venturia shut and bolted the door behind the departing Wardens. 'These two deal with spies and enemy agents; as I said, they're Zed Wardens. They don't know much about trade. Bet you they'll get on to headquarters, though, and before we know where we are, there'll be a couple of heavies from the External Trade Section banging on the door. And they won't be fooled.'

Hal grinned at Jouri. 'Was that all made up? About the pipe connectors and so on?'

'Oh, not entirely,' said Jouri. 'I do trade in such things. The Vemorians are crazy about water systems. Anything to do with controlling water flow, or canals or drainage or irrigation, and they're interested.'

'Good cover,' said Hal reflectively.

'Cover?' said Jouri innocently.

'For a spy,' said Hal.

Jouri raised a merry eyebrow. 'That's my trade,' he agreed. 'But I don't talk about it.'

'We don't want to know about it,' said Gilly quickly, quelling Hal with a look. Hal did want to know about it; she could tell he was bursting with questions. 'It isn't safe to know,' she said warningly. 'Not for Jouri or for us.'

'Quite right,' said Jouri. 'We'll say no more about it.'

Venturia surged back into the room. 'Food,' she said. 'Then as much sleep as possible for everyone. You must be up and away at first light. I can see trouble ahead.'

Early meant early, much to Hal's horror. He had slept soundly, without dreaming, exhausted at the end of a day that seemed to have lasted about as long as a normal week.

'Or even as long as a dull term at school,' he said to Gilly as he yawned his way up the stairs.

Gilly, lying under an enormous white-covered quilt, hadn't fallen asleep as quickly as Hal. She was in a tiny room under the eaves which contained nothing more than a high bed, with a thick mattress and carved wooden head and foot boards, and a gaily striped rug on the wide, polished wooden floorboards.

She could see the clear, dark sky through the little window. The stars shone with unusual brilliance; no pollution, thought Gilly. Could it really be that, in another place, it was still late morning of an August day, with a hot sun beating down on the castle? Could all this be happening while no time was passing there? Or had time passed there as well, were her frantic parents desperately looking for her and Hal?

Gilly knew that there was nothing she could do about it, but it seemed a long time until she fell asleep. Then she seemed only to have been asleep for a few minutes when she woke to find the stars and darkness gone, and the window a square of pale dawn light. A voice was calling up the narrow staircase which led to her room.

Venturia, telling her to get up, now, quickly; they had to be off.

Everything was done in a hurry. Venturia told them there was no time for breakfast, but she handed Jouri a basket of food.

'You can eat once you're on your way.'

The donkeys had been brought out of their stable and stood sleepily, heads down as Jouri and Lugh loaded them up. Lugh and Hal took the big basket inside, and went upstairs to get the head.

Gilly and Jouri couldn't help laughing at the torrent of abuse from the raven as it followed the head downstairs. Several windows were open, and the raven was screeching and protesting at the top of her very loud voice.

'If that bird doesn't shut its beak,' said Venturia, 'I'm going to silence it permanently, sacred bird or no sacred bird. Why the head had to bring it with him on this trip, I can't imagine.'

'Company,' suggested Gilly, still laughing.

'Company!' said Venturia scornfully. 'What kind of company is that!'

'Annoying company,' said Jouri as Lugh and Hal emerged, carefully carrying the head between them. They took no notice of the raven's alternate cursings and commands, nor of the head's imperious demands to know where he was being taken.

Lugh hoisted the head, oozing blood again, and by now with very dirty hair, into the basket. Gilly couldn't repress a shudder.

'It looks terrible,' she said. 'Why hasn't he healed up at all?'

Hal looked down at the head and pulled a face. 'He *is* a bit gory,' he admitted. 'I don't know where all the blood's coming from. I suppose if you're a god, even a minor one, you don't work the same as the rest of us.'

'The rest of us would be dead if our heads were cut off, for a start,' said Lugh.

Venturia appeared at the doorway, gesturing to them to hurry. 'People will be stirring soon. You must be away from here before the Wardens come back.'

'Won't they just follow us?' asked Gilly, falling in to

the convoy which clipped and clopped towards the outer door.

'Not at once,' said Jouri. 'Venturia will put them off the scent, and say we've gone north. Since that's the way they'd expect us to go if we're up to no good, they'll believe her.'

'And which way are we going?' asked Gilly.

'South-west,' said Venturia. She leant down and gave Gilly a hug. 'Goodbye, my dear. Keep your courage up, and remember, nothing will be asked of you that you can't do.'

With which cryptic words, she shut the door behind them.

Gilly didn't like the sound of that at all. Ominous, she thought; but you couldn't be worried for long, not on a crisp, clear morning like this, the air so fresh you could almost eat it.

They set off at a good pace, going back to where they had come off the main way, and then diving down another small street.

'Where are we going?' asked Hal, taking longer strides to catch up with Jouri, who was at the front of the column with his donkey.

'To Galat,' said Jouri.

'Galat?'

'The capital of Vemoria,' said Lugh from his post at the head of the other donkey. He sounded surprised. 'Is that a good idea?'

'They won't expect it,' said Jouri, 'and surprise is always good tactics. Besides, any cross-country journey would be very difficult. It makes more sense to go to Galat and then to leave by a different way to go towards the Walled city.'

'Is it a long way?' asked Gilly from the rear.

'Long way, of course it is, of course it is,' said the

raven, who had been mercifully silent until now, busy as she was with her early-morning preening. 'We must go by water, by water.'

'We are going by water,' said Jouri. 'Anything else would make the Vemorians really suspicious. Everyone goes to Galat by water. Nobody will notice us.'

Gilly and Hal had their doubts about this. They felt conspicuous, even though Venturia had seen to it that they were wearing the tunics and cloaks that everyone in Tuan and Vemoria seemed to wear. The cloak wasn't worn long, swinging free from the shoulders, but draped round and flung back over the right shoulder.

'Don't throw it back over your left shoulder, not in Vemoria,' Jouri warned them. 'Slaves wear them over their left shoulders, so it isn't a good idea.'

The air didn't seem quite so fresh to Gilly, suddenly. Slaves, she thought. Here in Vemoria, where we are. And we're going to the capital, the centre of this strange and not very friendly country.

'Penny for them,' said Hal.

She gave him a quick smile. 'Just nerves.'

Hal spoke with feeling. 'I think we've a lot to be nervous about.'

Fifteen

THE NARROW ROAD TURNED SUDDENLY TO THE left, and they found themselves on the waterfront. Hal and Gilly stood stock still in amazement. To them, canal meant holidays, leisurely afternoons on narrow strips of waterways, in a long boat, locks to be manoeuvred with care and patience.

This was quite different. For a start, it was wide, many times wider than any canal they had ever seen. Then, it was so busy. Barges, boats, and vessels of all kinds were tacking and sailing their way steadily up and down. One vessel came past at a fair pace, hauling six big, flat barges behind it, each one piled high with boxes.

'Strange sails,' said Hal. 'Look, Gilly, square, not triangular. All set at different angles, and quite small.'

'Gives a lot of control,' said Jouri, glancing at a slim boat with a huge number of sails which was sweeping past them. 'State Messenger, that one, they go at a terrific lick.'

'What happens when there isn't any wind?' asked Hal, still fascinated by the boats and their sails.

'There are always winds and breezes in Vemoria,' said Jouri. 'Some countries call it the Land of a Thousand Winds. The Vemorians don't like that name, it's too poetic for them. Here we are,' he added, as they came to a small quay where three flat boats were moored. One had a boatman sitting peacefully at the stern, smoking a pipe. He raised a hand in greeting to Jouri.

Jouri jumped down into the boat, and said something to the boatman, who nodded his head. There was a clink of coins, and then the boatman knocked his pipe out on the side of the boat and stood up.

Jouri came back to the others. 'That's all right,' he said. 'I've been on this boat before.'

The boatman had set up a ramp from the quay down into the boat. Jouri took hold of his donkey's bridle and led it down the ramp. It was clearly used to this, stepping neatly into the wide space in the centre of the boat. Its big ears flopped forward as it saw a bundle of hay tucked into a wooden rack.

Jouri went back to help Lugh. Pretending to tighten a strap, he bent over, and spoke to the head in its basket. 'I'm going to cover you; not a word, this is very dangerous territory as far as you're concerned.'

The raven opened her beak to express her disapproval, but Jouri caught her deftly round the claws. 'That means you, too. One squawk out of line, and you're in the pot. This is Vemoria, and talking ravens aren't good news here. Anything strange or magical, and you're in dead trouble. And when I say dead, I mean dead. OK?'

The boatman looked doubtfully at the raven as Jouri handed her over to a reluctant Hal.

'Nasty-looking bird, that. Pet, is it? You can teach them to talk, I've heard. Say "hello", that kind of thing.'

'Not this one,' said Jouri. 'It's a very stupid bird.'

The raven gave Jouri a ferocious look from her penetrating black eyes, but Jouri took no notice. He was too busy trying to persuade Lugh's donkey to go aboard the boat.

'That donkey,' Gilly said to Hal, 'doesn't want to do anything that anybody wants it to do.'

'Mmm,' said Hal, 'I know the feeling.'

They pushed, thumped, coochy-cooed at the donkey; all to no avail. Jouri was getting worried and kept looking anxiously back the way they had come. The area along the front of the canal was beginning to come to life. There were more barges and boats on the river, casements were being opened, and a few people were beginning to come out of the houses.

'The Wardens will be about now,' Jouri said under his breath.

Lugh caught the words. 'Not the Night Wardens, they'll have gone off duty.'

'Yes, and a nice fresh lot, full of zeal and enthusiasm, will be coming on duty, with their first job of the day being to come and get us for further questioning. We must get away!'

Hal took a step forward, looked thoughtfully at the donkey and then slipped on to the boat. He pulled out a handful of hay from the basket where Jouri's donkey was munching happily, and held it out invitingly to the other donkey. Its ears pricked, its head came up, and it trotted quickly and neatly on to the boat. Hal patted it and showed it the hay.

'Phew,' said Jouri, letting out a long breath. 'Well done, Hal.'

They clambered down into the boat and made their way past the donkeys. The boatman, inspired by the promise of a large tip for a speedy journey, rapidly cast off, and manoeuvred the boat away from the bank with his long pole.

They were on their way.

'This,' said Gilly, 'is wonderful.'

The others agreed. They weren't out of danger, in fact, they were heading for an extremely dangerous place, but for the moment they were safe. And who could feel worried or miserable, with the sparkling water running under the bows, the sails fluttering and filling with a pleasant breeze, the sun shining on endless green and yellow fields? They passed little villages, each with their network of canals running off the main one. Some of them had no roads or paths at all, just houses with bridges over the little waterways to the next patch of land with its house on it.

'Breakfast,' said Jouri, diving into the basket which Venturia had given them. Gilly realized how hungry she was as she bit into a crunchy bread roll. How could it be so fresh?

'Bakers open early in Vemoria,' said Jouri. 'They deliver along the canals.'

'Venturia's house wasn't on a canal,' pointed out Hal.

'It was,' said Jouri. 'At the back.'

'So why didn't we leave from there?'

'It was probably being watched,' said Lugh. 'If the Wardens were as suspicious as Jouri thinks, they'll have asked some of the householders there to keep an eye on Venturia's house.'

Gilly thought for a moment. 'But the Wardens didn't arrive at the back, they came to the door on to the pathway, the one we used.'

'They do, for checking records at night,' said Jouri. He lowered his voice. 'The boatmen aren't altogether keen on the Wardens,' he said. 'Boatmen keep their own ways and live by their own rules, as far as they can. The country wouldn't function without them, so they get away with quite a lot. The Wardens wouldn't trust them, though, especially at night.'

Gilly looked at their boatman with new respect. Hal was more practical. 'You mean this boatman might not tell the Wardens we were on his boat?'

'Exactly,' said Jouri.

Noise came from the basket, gurgling, hiccuping sounds. The boatman turned his head to see what was happening. Hal gave a loud belch – he was very good at that. 'Sorry,' he said. 'Fresh bread, it affects my stomach.'

Lugh slid casually over to where the head was lodged in its basket. The raven was balanced on the side of the boat, hopping from claw to claw in a particularly infuriating way. Lugh flapped his hand at the raven to get it to move and then bent down beside the basket.

He pretended he was adjusting his shoe. 'What's the matter?'

Gurgle.

Hal crouched down beside Lugh. 'What is it?' he said.

'Seasick,' said Lugh. 'I think he's seasick.'

'Seasick!' said Hal in his normal voice. Lugh made a furious gesture at him to keep his voice down.

'Sorry,' said Hal, this time in a whisper. 'How can he be seasick? This is a canal, it's as flat as anything. Besides, he hasn't got a stomach.'

'Must be upsetting his ears, the motion,' said Gilly, joining them. 'We did it in biology. There's fluid in the inner ear, and when it slops about in the wrong way, you feel sick.'

'Could be,' said Hal.

'He might still feel as though he's got a stomach. Like people who've had a leg amputated.'

— 130 —

'But he's a god,' said Hal. 'Whoever heard of a god being seasick?'

'Well, you have now,' said Gilly. 'We'll have to shut him up; if he goes on like this, the boatman's going to know we've got something a bit strange in the basket.'

Hal was feeling argumentative. 'Let him whinge on. We can say we've got a chicken in there.'

Unable to restrain herself, the raven let out a great caw of indignation. 'Take care, o miserable earth-dweller, how you speak of the god-head, yes, god-head.'

The boatman swung round, his eyes popping out of his head.

'Here, I thought you said that bird didn't talk.'

Hal stood up. 'It doesn't, but I'm trying to see if I can make it speak. Lugh here has only tried "Hello" and "Who's a pretty bird?" I thought it might do better with something more serious, so I'm trying.'

'Didn't sound like a boy speaking,' said the boatman astutely. 'Sounded like a man's voice.'

'Hal's voice is breaking,' Gilly said quickly. 'They teach him at school to speak like that, in a special voice. Because of it being poetry.'

'Poetry!' said the boatman, losing interest. 'Poetry! We boatman haven't got time for poetry!'

'Give the head a bit of air,' said Gilly softly to Lugh. 'Pull the cloth away. If we sit here, the boatman won't notice anything, and besides, look at all these boats. He'll bump into something if he doesn't concentrate.'

Trying to ignore the very nasty noises the head was making, Lugh did as Gilly suggested, and pulled the covering cloth back from the top of the basket to let in some air. The ghastly gurgles subsided very quickly into what sounded merely like poor plumbing, and in a few minutes, all they could hear was the odd hiccup.

'How long will it take us to get to Vemoria?' Gilly asked Jouri.

'About three hours,' said Jouri.

'You could get used to this,' said Hal, settling himself comfortably back against the curved side of the boat, and stretching out his legs. 'Very peaceful.'

'Enjoy it while you can,' said Jouri. 'I don't reckon things are going to stay peaceful. Quite the contrary. I don't think the Wardens will let us alone.'

'Jouri,' said Gilly, 'why are you so worried about the Wardens? What have we done that makes them so suspicious? Weren't the papers all right? Is it because we were staying with Venturia?'

'It's because you're young and not from Vemoria. Mab slipped out last night and listened to the Wardens talking about you.'

'Mab,' said Gilly, sitting up abruptly. 'We've forgotten Mab. We'll have to go back.'

'No, Mab'll find us if she wants to,' said Lugh, yawning. 'This sun and the water's making me very sleepy.' He settled himself down more comfortably.

'What did Mab hear?' Gilly asked Jouri.

'It seems there's an alert out. For two youngsters that have come through from another world.'

Gilly nudged Lugh with her foot, and dug an elbow into Hal's side. Annoyed, they opened their eyes and looked at her crossly.

'Cut it out, Gilly,' said Hal. 'Just because you never sleep in the daytime, it doesn't mean that everyone else has to stay awake.'

'Listen to what Jouri's saying. The Wardens know we've come through.' She turned back to Jouri. 'How can they know? Only Lugh and you and Mab know. And Venturia.'

Jouri looked thoughtful. 'Mab says óne of the others who came through has talked. The girl.'

'Erica!' said Hal. 'She would, of course.'

'They may have threatened her,' said Gilly, trying to be fair.

'No, I don't think so,' said Jouri. 'She's been here before, I reckon. Mab says she went straight off to report to the Twelve. Which is strange behaviour.'

'Very,' said Hal.

'Especially since she came through in a different place from you. The boy was hauled off at once; the Vemorians are terrified of people coming through. But not her. Honoured guest, so Mab says. Whoever she is, she told the authorities about you two. So the hunt is up.'

'If they've got Erica, they'll soon wish they hadn't,' said Hal.

'Oh, shut up, Hal,' said Gilly. 'What do they do with people who've come through, Jouri? Come on, I want to know. You said Bram was working on the canals.'

'They question them,' said Jouri reluctantly. 'If they answer straight away, and they believe them, then they just send them off to work as slaves. If they aren't sure about where you've come from, or it's from a place they aren't too worried about, then they wouldn't send you off to the stone quarries or anything like that.'

'Oh,' said Gilly. 'Good.'

'The stone quarries are where we'll all end up,' said Lugh, 'if we don't manage to get this head to the Walled City. Time enough to worry about your cousins when we've done that.'

'I think we ought to find Bram and rescue him first,' said Gilly obstinately.

'No way,' said Hal. 'Don't be stupid, Gilly. Our only chance is to get Pretty Face there to the Walled City, and hope that he keeps his word. Otherwise, we're all done for.'

Gilly had to agree. Besides, they had no idea where Bram was, so they could hardly rush to his rescue.

Jouri knew that it would be easy enough to find out exactly where Bram was, since even in Vemoria, people would gossip about a boy who had come through. He kept this fact to himself, though. He didn't want anything to get in the way of their getting the head to the Walled City. After they'd done that, well, then they would see.

He needed to take their minds off the subject. 'Right, you two,' he said in a brisk voice. 'I'm going to brief you about the Gonelands. If you're supposed to be from there, you'd better know something about it.'

Hal groaned. 'Not geography,' he said. 'I hate geography.'

Sixteen

'THE SCENERY'S CHANGING,' SAID HAL, looking across to the bank with half-closed eyes. Then he woke up properly from his doze and sat up to gaze at the surrounding countryside. 'More houses. Bigger ones. Fewer fields. Are we nearly there?'

'Lovely gardens,' said Gilly.

Jouri stretched and yawned. 'Yes, we're in the outskirts of Galat. Won't be long now. I must say, the boatman's made very good time.'

'Wow!' said Gilly, as they passed a palatial white house, with wonderful formal gardens reaching to the bank. 'Is it all like this?'

'No,' said Jouri. 'This is an area where a lot of rich families live.'

'Such as the Twelve?' asked Hal.

'That's it,' said Jouri. 'It's much more crowded on the other side, and much less grand.'

'Strange stone these houses are built of,' said Hal, who was interested in buildings. 'It's white, but it has a purple tinge to it. I've never seen anything like it.'

'That's the local stone,' said Jouri. 'Most of Galat is built of it. There are huge quarries over to the east of the country.'

'Worked by slaves,' said Lugh in a flat voice.

'You're looking very gloomy, Lugh,' said Gilly.

Lugh sighed. 'When I look at all this, and I think of

our towns and villages in Tuan – well, I don't think we've got a chance. Not against people who've got all this. No wonder they can equip their armies in the way they do.'

Jouri shot a warning look at the boatman, but he was intent on weaving his way through the ever-thickening river traffic and didn't seem to be listening.

'The Tuans have magic,' he reminded Lugh in a whisper.

'Not any more they don't,' hissed back Lugh.

'They will again, if we're successful,' said Hal.

'If,' said Lugh.

Jouri got up. He looked rested and back to his normal merry self again. He gave Lugh a cheerful smile as he held out a hand to help him up. 'No time for Ifs,' he said. 'Let's go and get the donkeys loaded up. We need to be off this boat and away into the city as quickly as possible.'

Hal got up as well, earning himself a 'Chut' of rebuke from the boatman as the boat lurched slightly.

'Sorry,' said Hal. 'Come on, Gilly, nearly there.'

'We won't be staying long in Galat, will we?' Gilly said as she tossed her cloak over her shoulder, remembering to do it the right way.

'Shouldn't think so,' said Hal. 'I expect we'll press on to the Walled City as quickly as poss.'

He was about to go and help the other two, but Gilly held him back for a moment. 'What about Bram and Erica, Hal? What if they're here in Galat? We must try to find them. Just think how they'd feel if we got back home and said we'd mislaid them in another world.'

Hal pulled a face. 'Yes, I can see that going down a treat,' he said. 'Although I can't see anyone minding about Erica.'

'Hal!' said Gilly. 'Her parents would miss her.'

'I should think she must drive them crazy,' said Hal unrepentantly. 'But even if you're right, I think we've got to do this business with the head first, Gilly. That's why we're here, as far as I can see. Maybe, if Lugh gets his powers back, and if there are any other Tuans around, then they can help us to find the others. I don't see what we can do by ourselves here in Galat, where we're total strangers.'

'Not just strangers,' said Gilly. 'Aliens, really.'

'I suppose we are,' said Hal, struck by the idea. 'Like Martians.'

'Only without the antennae or the green skins.'

'Might as well have them,' said Hal. 'I don't think we blend at all.'

In that, Hal was mistaken. Galat was a world away from the country area where Venturia lived.

'It's Vemoria being so powerful and successful these days,' explained Jouri, as they made their way through bustling streets. 'People come from all over, for work and to do business, pick up new ideas, find out what's going on. It is the capital, after all.'

Hal and Gilly were relieved to find how unnoticeable they were among the throng of people. There was a core of what were clearly Vemorians, easily spotted by the way they held themselves, straight and unyielding, by their air of confidence and pride, as well as their heavy, well-made tunics and cloaks. In comparison, many of the other people they saw coming and going looked as though they were dressed up for a fancy-dress party. Vivid colours, long tunics, strange headgear, great swirling robes . . .

'I don't think anyone would spot us,' Gilly said to Hal, as she struggled to keep beside him.

Hal wasn't really listening, he was drinking in the colourful life around him. He was fascinated by the shops with their goods stretching out on to the sidewalk, and by the alert shopkeepers calling to them to inspect their wares. Other traders leapt forward, asking what they had to sell, demanding to see what they had in their baskets, eager to make offers for whatever it was. Lugh had to walk along beside the pannier, holding the top down, hoping that none of the inquisitive merchants would get too close and find themselves trying to buy more than they had bargained on.

'Fetch a fortune, that head,' said Jouri under his breath in a wistful voice, his own trading instincts coming to the fore. 'Set us up for life.'

'Don't even think of it,' said Lugh.

They had several good offers for the raven, although they were unsure whether the would-be purchasers wanted to buy the bird to eat or to keep as a pet. Privately, Hal thought it was an excellent chance to get rid of the tiresome creature, with her endless nagging ways, but Gilly pointed out that the minute she opened her beak, the game would be up.

'She'll probably strike up at any moment and get us all arrested in any case,' said Hal. 'We should have dumped her in the other basket, it would have been much safer.'

The raven heard, as they could tell from the malevolent glance she shot at them. Fortunately, the head had told her to keep quiet if she ever wanted to see him in one piece again, and she was obeying orders, although clearly storing up a list of complaints for later reference.

'Aren't people always falling into the canals?' Gilly asked Jouri.

'Only strangers,' said Jouri. 'All the locals are used to them, and of course all the Vemorians grow up alongside water. Either they drown when they're very little, or they learn. Mostly, they learn. Here in Galat, they have Street Watchers. They keep an eye on everything and everyone – it's a paid job, fat wages from the State – and they have special poles for helping out anyone who falls in. They also have to make sure shopkeepers and householders keep the water clean. They don't want the waterways clogged up with everyone's rubbish.'

'I wouldn't have thought the Vemorians were very rubbishy sort of people,' said Gilly.

'No,' agreed Jouri. 'But a lot of shopkeepers and merchants aren't Vemorians, so they need watching. Look, there's one of the Street Watchers up there, standing on the bridge.'

The narrow canals with their wide pavements on either side were crossed at regular intervals by strange little bridges, which rose to a point in the middle. Sure enough, a glum figure was posted on the one that Jouri had nodded towards.

'Don't like the look of him,' said Hal, keeping his head down. 'Are you always being watched here?'

'Yes,' said Jouri. 'And listened to. You have to assume that someone is picking up everything you say.'

'Even now?' said Hal.

'Even as we speak,' said Jouri, making a snatch at a young boy who was walking nonchalantly along beside them.

The boy ducked, and pulled a rude face at them. 'What you got in that basket, then?' he asked, his eyes flickering over the pannier. 'It's alive. Have you got a licence for it?'

Jouri made another grab at him, but the boy slipped easily out of reach and darted away down a narrow passageway.

Jouri glanced at the basket. The boy was right; despite their best efforts, the Head's eyes were gleaming, unmistakably alive and quite clearly not the eyes of a rabbit or a chicken, such as a respectable farmer in from the country might be carrying.

'That boy's gone off to report us,' said Jouri. 'We'll have to hurry.'

By dint of much shoving and pushing and dragging of the donkeys, they managed to go faster. Jouri went ahead, leading them away from the more crowded centre where they had landed into quieter alleyways with only the occasional shop, although still, always, the dark thread of water ran in a central channel.

They came unexpectedly to a small square. Four canals met here, in a central pool with a grim little statue at its centre. Jouri led the way smartly across three of the four little pointy bridges, ducked through an archway into another, waterless square, and immediately vanished from view.

The rest of the party stopped, unsure which way to go. Then Hal spotted Jouri, his finger on his lips, standing half way up a broad flight of stairs. He gestured to the wide doors beneath, and Lugh judged, rightly, that they were to take the donkeys through there. Jouri gave a soft tap on a door behind him, and slipped into the darkness within, as it opened and shut again before anyone could notice.

Hal gave the door a tentative push, and it opened instantly on smooth hinges. Lugh hauled the donkeys inside, helped by Gilly pushing from behind. Hal quickly swung the doors to, and leant back against them as he looked about him.

They were in a courtyard garden. Not a courtyard like Venturia's, which was a working yard, with chickens and farm equipment. This was a place to relax in, with slender pillars supporting arches round three sides, a fountain in the middle, and a riot of colour from flowering plants which grew everywhere. The air was thick with their scent.

Gilly gave an 'Oh!' of surprise, and then shut her eyes, breathing in the wonderful smells and relishing the warm sun on her face.

Hal looked round with interest. 'This isn't a bit like anything else we've seen in Galat,' he said to Lugh. 'All the buildings we've seen have been so . . .' He couldn't think of exactly the way to describe the massive, impressive but austere buildings which marched along the canals, as severe and immovable as the native citizens seemed to be.

'I think this is part of the old Vemoria,' said Lugh. 'Before the Twelve took over. Nothing was so orderly then. I remember one of my uncles telling me about it. I wonder how this has survived. My uncle said they set out to pull down all the old, irregular houses, and built new ones – like all the ones we've come past.'

Gilly's attention was caught. 'Do you mean the Vemorians weren't always like this?' she asked.

'No, not at all,' said Lugh. 'A long time ago, all these lands were ruled by the Old Kings. They were quite budsy-wudsy with the Tuan Old Kings, they were all related. Then there was some trouble, a rebellion of some kind. That was when Vemoria and Tuan started to go their separate ways and the First Rulers took over. They were magicians. It wasn't until the First

—— 141 ——

Rulers were overthrown by the Twelve, though, that Vemoria became like it is now.'

'Ah, the twelve families that you told us about yesterday.'

'Yes, Vemoria is an oligarchy, ruled by those families. Cold, clever, powerful men and women. Just the sort you'd know would rule a state like Vemoria.'

While he was talking, Lugh had pulled the basket off the donkey, and he took the cover off to give the head some air. Hal went over to give him a hand.

The head spoke. He sounded sulky, but dangerously so; a rich, menacing sulkiness, Gilly thought uneasily.

'The Twelve took over about a hundred and fifty years ago, by your reckoning of time,' said the head. 'Things have got worse ever since.'

Lugh was indignant. 'Some of your immortal friends helped the Twelve to come to power. Or that's what everyone says,' he added, seeing the great eyes glaring at him through the basket.

'Take me out of here,' said the head. 'I've had enough of it. It smells.'

'That's the blood,' said Gilly helpfully, and got a hostile glare for her pains.

'I will no longer travel in that,' said the head, as Lugh gingerly caught him under the chin and carefully eased him out of the basket.

The raven had swooped up to the steeply slanting roof to survey the neighbourhood. She came down and landed beside the head with a great flutter of wings. 'There are people coming,' she announced croakily. 'Yes, people coming. Down the streets. Wardens. Officials. What a shame, what a shame, what a shame. That peasant friend of yours—'

'If you mean Jouri,' Lugh began, but the Raven took no notice.

' – that peasant, I say, has brought the god-head into danger. Yes, into danger.'

Hal was quite ready to argue the point, since, as a matter of fact, it was the head who had landed them all in danger.

There wasn't time for an argument. To Gilly's great relief, a door on the fourth side of the garden flew open, and a tall, thin man with a shock of white hair came out, with Jouri at his side.

He gave a quick glance at the donkeys, at Lugh, still standing by the head, which he had propped up against a pillar, and at Hal and Gilly. He snapped his fingers, and a young man, dressed in dark red clothes, appeared instantly at his side. The old man said something to him in a low voice, and the man nodded in agreement. He gave a quick, casual bow to Lugh and the others, and then, taking the halters, swept the donkeys away through an arch and out of sight. The old man sketched a formal greeting to the head, and with no more ado, picked it up.

'He must be strong,' said Gilly, amazed. 'You know how heavy that head is.'

'Bring the baskets,' he said. 'Raven, follow me.'

He ushered them towards the door as a lot more people, all dressed in the same dark red clothes, came quickly into the yard, wheeling what looked like pieces of high fencing. They placed them in grooves which ran, so Hal noticed for the first time, in a rectangle inside the front part of the garden. Arches, pillars, flowers and fountain were all obscured by the plain walls.

'Come,' said the old man. 'The Wardens will be here at any minute.'

He led them along a winding passage and up a spiral staircase. At the top was an octagonal room, windowless, but comfortably furnished with benches and seats, all covered in rich cloths and ornately patterned cushions.

'Wait here until they've gone,' the man said. 'Wylith will get you some refreshments.'

Hal and Gilly looked at each other and then at Lugh and Jouri.

'Who is he?' said Hal. 'Why is he helping us? What was all that in the garden?'

The man called Wylith set a tray with goblets and a slender glass jug on the table in front of them. Hal and Gilly liked the look of Wylith. He didn't seem to be much older than they were, and he looked as though he laughed a lot.

'When the Wardens search, they'll come through the big doors to find a well-appointed shed,' he told them.

'Won't they be suspicious, if it's empty?' asked Gilly.

Wylith grinned. 'It won't be,' he said. 'By now it will be full of all the things the Wardens would expect to find in a neat and tidy Vemorian out-house. Then they'll search the rest of the building. Of course, they won't find anything. The master will see to that.'

'The master?' said Hal.

'You saw him just now. He's very good at keeping the Wardens happy; he's had years of practice.'

Wylith handed out glasses of a clear, sparkling liquid with slices of fruit floating on the surface. He arrived at the head, which the old man had placed carefully on a seat to itself. Wylith bowed. 'Lord, can you drink?' he asked.

The head glowered at him. 'You may wet my lips,' he said disagreeably.

Wylith raised an eyebrow, whisked out a clean white handkerchief, dipped it into a glass of the liquid and touched the head's mouth with it.

'*Tergom*,' said the head. 'This is *tergom*. How does your master come by this?'

Wylith laughed. 'He is a descendant of the First Rulers, Lord. He has always drunk *tergom*, and served it to honoured guests.' He bowed gracefully. 'Such as yourself.'

The head wasn't impressed. 'Yes, and to riff-raff like this lot, what a waste. I don't believe you, in any case. The man is an impostor, there are none of the First Rulers' families left.'

Wylith bowed again. 'As you say, Lord.'

That annoyed the head. 'I would know, wouldn't I? I'm a god, we of the Third Lands know everything that goes on here. In fact, we—'

He stopped abruptly.

'In fact, we manipulate it?' said Wylith helpfully and politely, but with a glint in his eye.

The head passed its tongue across its lips and said nothing.

The raven, as usual, had plenty to say.

'Stupid boy, stupid boy, you understand nothing. Silence before a great one, who are you to ask questions of him? And stupid questions, too, irrelevant and stupid questions.'

'Does it always go on like this?' said Wylith, putting the tray down, and staring at the raven.

'That's nothing,' said Hal. 'It's a ghastly nag, on and on. And you can't answer back, because it just starts squawking and cawing about the god-head. I don't know how he puts up with it.'

The raven opened her beak and let out a crowing howl. 'Without me,' she said, her voice dark with rage, 'without me, this task cannot be completed. Silence, you dross of the earth. Silence, I say.'

Wylith watched with interest. 'Of course, it's a sacred bird,' he said. 'Nothing you can do with them, but it doesn't make them any the less tiresome. My master had one once, and were we glad when she took herself off on some mission. Never came back, thank goodness.'

'Sacred bird?' said the raven, cocking its head on one side and sidling along the curtain rail. 'What sacred bird is this?'

'Nothing, nothing,' said Wylith hastily. 'Not your kind of sacred, just a pet.'

He took up the tray, placed it on the central table, and bowed towards the head.

Then his expression changed. They could see he was attentive, listening, catching some sound which they couldn't see.

'Trouble?' said Lugh.

Wylith nodded. 'I'm afraid so.' He frowned. 'I don't see how they can have broken through the magic—'

'Magic?' said Jouri, his eyebrows raised. 'Here? In Vemoria?'

'Oh, there's plenty of magic in Vemoria. Old magic, you know. It's kept well-hidden—' He broke off. 'I don't understand . . . I must go. You stay here and guard that head.'

'I'll come with you,' said Jouri, 'at once.'

'And so will I,' said Lugh. 'You two, stay here with the head.'

'You're safe here,' said Wylith. 'This tower is bound with the strongest magic of all.'

Hal started to protest. 'But can't we—'

—— 146 ——

They didn't stay to listen, but went quickly out of the room. The door closed noiselessly behind them.

'On our own, then,' said Gilly.

'Yes,' said Hal.

'What a shame, what a shame, what a shame,' said the raven.

Seventeen

'I DON'T LIKE THE SOUND OF THAT,' SAID HAL. His sharp ears had caught some distant and not very peaceful sounds. He put his glass of *tergom* down and went to the door, still listening. He opened it, and then jumped back, startled.

An enormous black cat with a sleek coat and huge greeny-gold eyes came into the room. Not in the usual I've-got-all-the-time-in-the-world way of cats, but in a hasty, ruffled way. It looked round, and then backed towards the door, head up, tail weaving backwards and forwards.

Gilly stared at it, not much liking the look of the animal. It was too big for a domestic cat for a start, being more the size of a small panther, she thought. A panther with some very sharp-looking claws at the end of its large paws.

'It's purring,' said Hal, as a growling sound emerged from the cat's throat.

'Growling,' said Gilly.

'Caw,' said the raven. 'Get it out of here, out of here.' Sacred she might be, but she liked cats no better than her more everyday relatives did.

'No,' said Hal. 'I'm sure it's trying to tell us something, I don't think it's going to attack . . . and something is up out there, you can hear voices, and feet . . . an awful racket.'

The cat's tail swung from side to side. It eyed Hal, and then pounced, landing on his foot and grabbing him behind his ankle with its paw as though catching a mouse. It released him and headed for the door once more.

'I think you're right, Hal,' said Gilly with some relief. 'I don't think it wants to attack us at all. It wants us to follow it.'

'I'll get the head,' said Hal shortly. He dived towards the seat and, winding some of the horrid hair around his wrist to get a good hold, he heaved the head up.

The head gave a most ungodlike bellow. 'Let go at once, guttersnipe.'

Hal took no notice. 'Come on,' he said to Gilly. 'I don't think we've got much time.'

'What about Lugh?' she asked, holding the door open for him, and ducking as the raven shot through at head level, screeching and flapping her wings in indignation. 'And Jouri?'

'No time.'

There was a clatter of running footsteps, and shouting, now much nearer. In fact, from the sound of it there were people just along the stone passage at the foot of the spiral staircase.

The cat pushed past them, back into the chamber. Hal swung round to see what the cat was up to, almost falling down the stairs as he did so.

'Hal, oh, do be careful,' said Gilly.

The cat was clawing at one of the hangings beside the big chair where the head had rested. Hal and Gilly watched for a few brief seconds, and then realizing what the animal was up to, dashed forward to drag the heavy seat aside. They pulled the curtain back.

'A door!' said Gilly.

'Locked,' said Hal, desperately as he tried the

— 149 —

handle. He lunged against it with his shoulder, but it didn't move a millimetre.

Gilly darted to the other side of the room. There, on the table, where she had noticed it earlier half-hidden under a dish, was an old iron key.

'Try this.'

Hal tried, it turned, and the door swung open. A fusty, musty smell of long wilted flowers wafted out as they peered into the darkness. In a flash, the cat was through. Hal picked up the head again, the raven swooped past them. Gilly went last, closing the door firmly behind them, and turning the key in the lock.

The minute the door clicked to, the darkness became total. They inched forward, feeling in front of them with their hands. No barrier in front, and no walls to the sides.

'Where can we be?' Gilly whispered. 'It must be a hall or something. I hope we don't bump into any furniture.'

'It's so slow,' said Hal. 'Whoever's coming up those stairs will find the door in two seconds, and they'll be after us. And they don't have a great head weighing them down.'

Gilly stopped. 'Hal, we're outside.'

Hal's voice came out of the dark. 'How can we be? We must still be in the building; we were in a tower, we haven't gone down any steps. This must be a loft or something attached to one side of the tower.'

'It feels as though we're on grass,' said Gilly. 'And smell the air! It isn't stuffy at all now, and that musky scent has gone . . . it smells fresh.'

Hal sniffed the air. Gilly was right. And he could feel

the stirrings of a breeze on his cheek . . . and surely that was a faint rustling of leaves?

'It's getting light,' said Gilly.

It was. A rosy, dappled sunlight began to flicker through the branches which they could now quite clearly make out overhead.

Hal stopped abruptly, forgetting for a moment the weight of the head which was dragging him down with every step.

'Apples,' he said, awed.

Apples indeed, but not like any other apples which Hal and Gilly had ever seen. These were a pinky red, with gold tips, and they shone as though George, their local greengrocer, had been polishing them after giving them a good spit, the way he always did.

'George would love these,' said Gilly.

She was overcome suddenly with homesickness, with longing for everything to be normal, to wake up in her own bed, to go to the shops for her mother, to lie and read an Asterix in the garden while Hal idled in his hammock and the tie ropes went squeak, squeak as he swung gently to and fro . . .

There was no gentle squeak, just a raucous hoot from the raven, who was restored to her usual belligerent, nagging mode.

'You useless children, where have you brought us? You of another world, ignorant scum, who know nothing of our ways, lugging the god-head as though he was meat on the butchers slab . . . and to where? A garden. Go back at once, at once.'

'Oafs,' added the god-head, his eyes narrow slits of contempt. 'You will pay for this.'

'Back where?' said Hal, politely enough, but Gilly could hear the repressed laughter in his voice. It

—— 151 ——

cheered her up; if Hal felt like laughing, then things weren't probably so bad.

'Look around,' said Hal.

They looked. Apple trees, heavy with fruit, stretched to where the trees seemed so dense they could see no further. In the other direction, a low wall, and beyond it open fields, meadows . . . not a house or a person to be seen. The air had the hum of open country; bird calls, the quiet sound of insects, a faint stirring of leaves.

'No house,' said Gilly.

'No town,' said Hal, turning a full three hundred and sixty degrees, just to make sure.

'No canals,' said a familiar voice from overhead.

'Mab!' said Gilly, hugely relieved. 'Mab, it's you.'

'Yes,' said Mab, 'It's me, which is all very well, but how do I get down from this tree?'

'The same way you got up it,' suggested Hal, ever helpful.

'I was a cat, then,' said Mab crossly. 'You may have noticed.'

'You were the black cat!' cried Gilly.

'I was.'

'Why didn't you say anything? Why did you just wave your tail and bound about?'

'There's gratitude,' grumbled Mab, peering down through the branches to find a safe route down.

With some help from Hal and sarcastic squawks from the raven, Mab finally managed to slither to the ground.

'Poof,' she said. 'I'm too old for that kind of thing. Oh, it is good to be back in human shape again. Dogs, then a cat . . . you've no idea how itchy it is, fur, when you aren't used to it.'

'Why didn't you change back in there – wherever it was that we were?'

'Oh, I couldn't possibly have done that,' said Mab with a shudder. 'Mega magic there, far stronger than anything I can manage. Dear me, no.'

'What was going on in there, Mab?' asked Hal. 'Do you know? We're worried about Lugh. He went off with Wylith, and then we heard fighting.'

'Yes, the Wardens broke through the spell which kept the main part of the house out of reach – and has done so for many years. I can't think how they managed it, they must have had an informer. No, I don't know what's happened to Lugh, or Jouri, but I should think that Wylith will have got them away.'

'Why did the Wardens come?' asked Gilly.

'They were after you, I'm afraid,' said Mab. 'They've heard about the head, and I expect they managed to capture some of the Tuan villagers who didn't hotfoot it quite fast enough away from the new borders. A story about a dead god, and then the head business . . . well, no Tuan could resist telling a good tale like that. The Wardens would put two and two together, knowing that there are a couple of other-worlders on the loose and reported as having crossed into Vemoria . . .'

'How would they know?'

'Zed Wardens' report,' said Mab. 'And from your cousins, too, no doubt. It was bound to happen.'

'Mab,' said Hal. 'Mab, where are we?'

Mab looked around her and sighed.

'I mean, we were in that octagonal room, right up at the top of a tower, we went through a door, and now . . .'

Mab drifted over to a wall and they followed her, Hal making sure that the head, propped up against a tree, wasn't about to roll over. 'I hate him,' he whispered to Gilly, 'but it must be horrible, rolling over on your stump.'

'Serve him right,' said Gilly viciously. 'He's the cause of all our troubles. What is it, Mab?'

Mab was pointing across the meadows to where a river ran between green banks. 'Does that look familiar?'

'No,' said Hal at once.

'Yes it does,' said Gilly in the same moment. 'Look at the colour, Hal. It's like the canal we came to Galat on.'

Grudgingly, Hal admitted that it might be the case, but so what?

'Is it the same?' Gilly asked Mab.

Mab nodded. 'I think so. I think that door which I brought you through was a time door.'

'Time door?'

'Yes, I didn't know, or I would have . . . well, what else could I do? If we'd gone back down the stairs, you would have been captured, and the head taken.'

'How did you know there was a door?' Hal was suspicious. 'Have you been there before?'

'No,' said Mab. 'But all octagonal tower rooms like that have a hidden door somewhere. Or most of them, and since that was a very magical house, I thought there couldn't possibly only be one door.'

'You were right, and we're very grateful,' said Gilly.

'No, we're not,' said Hal. 'Out of the frying pan into the fire, I'd say.'

'What is a time door?' asked Gilly.

'She means we've come out into a different time, isn't that it, Mab?' said Hal shrewdly.

'I'm afraid so.'

'Another time?' Gilly couldn't believe it. 'But where

are we? Are we in another country? Are we even further from getting home?'

'No, I think we're in the same country, in fact, I think we're in exactly the same place.'

'Galat?' Hal didn't believe her.

'Galat will be built here, sometime in the future.'

Gilly was thinking. 'I do believe they had a tree like this in the courtyard,' she said. 'When we first arrived at the house.'

Mab nodded. 'One is supposed to have survived, and it wouldn't be surprising if it was there. This is the orchard of the Old Kings. Long since gone; once the Twelve took over in Vemoria and started getting everything the way they wanted, the orchards were all cut down.'

She paused and glanced at the head. 'You see, under the First Rulers, Galat was a city, but it was just a city on a river. A lot of the houses had gardens, and I suppose a lot of them would have had these apple trees in them. But the Twelve took over, and the gardens vanished along with the old buildings. They straightened the river and widened it, and built all the other waterways . . . These trees have a power, so it's said. The Vemorians wouldn't approve of that at all. They'd be a link with the Old Kings, definitely not on the Twelve's O.K. list.'

'If there's one tree still standing . . . In the courtyard, I mean.'

'It won't be by now,' said Mab shaking her head. 'Several of the watchers who had come to attack the building had axes. I think they knew exactly what to expect. The tree will have been hacked down and they'll burn it as soon as they can.'

'Bad news,' said Hal, looking at the ancient but beautiful trees around him. 'Do the apples taste good?'

He reached up as he spoke, and Mab let out an uncouth yell.

'No, Hal,' said Gilly, restraining him. 'You're hungry, I'm hungry, too, but I think nicking these apples is a bit beyond ordinary scrumping.'

'Why?' said Hal impatiently. 'There are masses of them, and it doesn't look as though there's anybody around to eat them. What a waste.'

'No windfalls,' said Gilly, looking at the ground under the trees. 'None at all.'

'They won't fall very often,' said Mab. 'Magic, of course. You're right, much better not to eat them. You never know with food, apples in particular. We might have to stay in this time for ever if we ate some.'

'Then desist.' The head's voice rang out from his spot under one of the biggest trees. 'Knaves! Fools! We must get back into our time at once.'

Hal bristled. 'Yes? And just how do we do that, loud-mouth?'

The raven soared into the air and flapped her wings in Hal's face. 'Your disrespect for a godly one will be punished, yes, punished, I say!'

'Never mind that,' said Gilly. 'Mab, can we get back? We must find Lugh. And I think we need to find our cousins, too. The more I hear about the Vemorians, the more I think they probably aren't having a very good time.'

Hal looked mulish. 'Nor are we,' he pointed out. 'And even if they are slaves, I don't suppose they'll come to any harm. Might even do that ghastly Erica some good. She'll have to shut up and listen to what other people want. She won't like that at all.'

'Hal, that isn't the point,' Gilly began.

'It certainly isn't the point,' boomed the head. 'Nothing matters, except to get me to the Walled City and bury me, so that I can be reunited with my body and go back beyond the Spellbound Gorge.'

'So that we Tuans can all get our magic powers back,' said Mab, very forcefully for her.

'Oh, well, yes. I suppose so, that was the agreement,' said the head without much enthusiasm. 'But it is I, the god-head, who matters. Everything else is but the meanderings of ants, creatures of no importance.'

'We can't stay here,' said Hal, paying absolutely no attention to the head's arrogant remarks.

'Why not?' said Gilly, in a sleepy voice. 'It's so lovely here. Warm, and so peaceful. One could just lie down and forget everything. For ever, and ever,' she added, her voice now sounding dreamy and far away.

There was a thump, and one of the apples fell to the ground. It rolled towards Gilly, who picked it up. As she did so, it crumbled and fell apart in her hand. Gilly looked at the remnants of flesh and seeds on her hand as though they were in the far distance.

Mab took one look at Gilly, then grabbed hold of her and shook her violently. To Hal's surprise, Gilly didn't react at all, she just smiled, her eyes closing.

'Out of here,' shouted Mab. 'Hal, quick, quick, we're losing her.'

'What . . . ?' Hal stared at Gilly.

'It's the magic, it's too strong, quick, away from the trees, out of the garden. Bring the head.'

Mab half dragged, half pushed the stumbling Gilly towards the low wall. Hal ran behind her, pulling the head along the ground by his hair. The raven, beside herself at the indignity of it all, cawed and flapped unhelpfully around their heads.

Mab reached the wall, and with a huge effort, got Gilly over it. Then she scrambled over herself, and

—— 157 ——

reached back to take the head. Between them, she and Hal got it over, followed by Hal, who didn't like the feeling of languor which was beginning to creep up his legs.

'Oof,' he said, landing with a thump beside the head, who was looking thunderous.

'Away from me, clod,' cried the head in his amiable way. Hal obligingly rolled over, and hauled himself into a sitting position. He looked around, surprised to find himself in the long grass of a very ordinary-looking meadow. Gilly, he saw, seemed to be waking up, although she still looked a bit blank.

'What was all that about?' he demanded of Mab, who was rubbing Gilly's hands.

'Not just an ordinary time door,' said Mab. 'In fact, I don't think a time door at all. Just very strong magic taking us temporarily out of time. Not forwards or backwards, or even sideways . . . simply out of time. Very dangerous.'

'So what happened to Gilly?'

Mab shrugged. 'I think both of you would have been overcome if we'd stayed any longer. It was some emanation from those trees.'

They both turned to look back at the garden. Hal let out a kind of yelp. Gone were the venerable trees with their glossy leaves and gleaming apples. All that was left were some twisted stumps and spiky branches, leafless and rotten, with a dull ivy creeping over them.

Mab shook her head. 'Very, very nasty,' she said. 'I think we need to get away from here as fast as we can.'

Hal gave Gilly a few friendly slaps to encourage her back to reality. 'That's all very well, Mab, but if we aren't in another time, just out of time – although I don't see how that explains those trees – then where are we? And where's Galat? And Lugh and Jouri? And the donkeys,' he added grimly, looking at the bulk of the head.

'We could do with a donkey,' agreed Mab. 'I don't know, Hal. I suspect we're in Galat, that's all around us, only we can't see them and they can't see us.'

Hal put his head in his hands. 'I can't take much more of this,' he said. 'Nothing is what it seems.'

'That's life,' said Mab cheerfully. 'Come on, Gilly, on your feet. We need to get going.'

'There's just one little problem,' said Hal. 'That head. Gilly and I can't manage him for more than a short way. Quite apart from being disgusting, and horrible to handle, he's extremely heavy. And he doesn't like being carried by his hair.'

'I demand a proper carrier,' said the head.

'Indeed, indeed,' squawked the raven. 'The god-head must have his due, his due.'

'Right,' said Hal, taking a swipe at the raven, which hopped smartly out of range. 'You tell us where we find a proper carrier, as your boss calls it.'

Mab had been thinking. 'If we could manage to get it down to the river bank,' she said, 'I can see that there are several promising-looking poles down there. We could make a firm knot in his hair—'

Growls of rage from the head.

' – and suspend him from it. Then you two can take an end of the pole each. No, Hal, I can't, I can't touch him, it could take away any magic I've got left. Permanently. Then where would we all be?'

'Actually,' Gilly told Mab. 'I don't think I could carry anything just at the moment, but I'll feel better if we get moving. Hal, can you haul the head as far as the river?'

The head had subsided back into the sulks, much to their relief, so Hal didn't have to put up with too much abuse as he manoeuvred it across the meadow and down the long, sloping sward of grass that led to the river. Gilly walked behind, ignoring the complaining and the raven, trying to keep her feet steady; not easy when your head is swimming.

They reached the river, and Gilly sank down gratefully beside the water, splashing it on to her face to revive herself. Hal and Mab walked over to where there were several poles of the kind they needed, lying close to the water's edge, and picked one which looked about the right length and seemed likely to be strong enough to carry the head.

Mab stood over Hal while he tied a rather clumsy but strong knot in the head's hair. It was thick and matted with dried blood, and Hal screwed up his face in distaste as he looked at the rusty stains on his hands and arms. 'Now I've got to get rid of this blood,' he grumbled, heading for a patch of grass.

'Use the river, idiot,' said Gilly, who was feeling more herself again.

Hal grinned, and sank down at the river's edge. He leant forward and idly watched the red stain from his hands seep out into the water.

His eyes widened as he saw how big the stain was becoming. There was no way he had got that much blood on him.

'Some blood,' he remarked, standing up and shaking the drops of water off him.

'Some stain,' said Mab, who had come up silently behind him. 'Look at the river.'

Before their astonished eyes, the blue-gold river was darkening to a rusty-red colour. 'A river of blood,' said Hal under his breath. At the same time the sky was growing rapidly darker, the sun quite blotted out, and the air around them was becoming grey-green, cold, clammy, ominous . . . and unbreathable.

'Mab,' Gilly called out. 'Where are you? Hal?'

Gasping for breath, they reached out and found each other, and clung together desperately.

'The head,' said Mab. 'We mustn't lose the head. At all costs we mustn't lose the head . . .'

Eighteen

'*B*IG MAC!'
Cough, splutter. Stinging eyes. It was the worst nightmare you ever had, wrapped all around you . . .

'Big Mac,' shrieked Mab again, in a voice thick from the yellow fog. 'With fries. Go ON. Think of REAL THINGS.'

Was it their imagination, or was the mist less thick?

'Awful car ads on the telly,' said Gilly, catching on.

'Ticket machines on the Underground,' said Hal.

Definitely less thick, and the air more breathable.

'Double-decked buses,' sang out Mab.

'Double decker,' mumbled Hal.

'It doesn't *matter*,' said Gilly. 'Sun cream.'

'Maths prep.'

'First day of the holidays.'

'Toothpowder.'

'What?'

'For cleaning your teeth.'

'Toothpaste, Mab.'

'No, powder. It comes in tins.'

'Only if you have false teeth, and . . . Oh, never mind. Indian takeaways.'

'Don't Hal, I'm so hungry. The Grand National . . .'

It had worked.

The mist had vanished, the sun was sparkling in the sky, and the river . . .

The river was no longer rust-red. But nor was it the tranquil natural river of before. Its edges were straighter, its banks further apart and no longer green. Shadows fell. Gone were the meadows and the grass and the willows on the bank. Here instead were wharves and warehouses. Boats plying to and fro. Bridges.

Watchers.

'I think we're back,' said Mab in subdued tones. 'We'll have to be very, very careful.'

Hal bit his lip. 'I think we need to be out of here as soon as we can.'

'Hire a boat,' screeched the raven. 'Hire a boat. Right away, right away.'

'Yes,' said the head. 'A boat. Let it be well-appointed and smooth-sailing, fit to carry a god-head.'

'We can't hire a boat,' said Hal. 'We haven't any money. Lugh has the money.'

'No money,' echoed the raven, far too loudly. 'No money. What a shame, what a shame, what a shame.'

'Shut up,' said Hal fiercely. They were in deep shadows at the moment, and the Watcher on the nearest bridge, not over-zealous by the look of him, was hanging over the parapet to chat to a friend. So far he hadn't noticed them.

Gilly had been examining her pockets. 'No money,' she said. 'Lugh had it. All I've got is some apple remains in my hanky.'

'Very useful,' said Hal. 'Now what?'

Gilly wasn't listening. She was watching a man on the other side of the canal. He was working with two other men and a boy, loading boxes on to a long flat boat. One of the men had a sheaf of papers, and was clearly checking items off on a list.

The boxes were finally heaped up to their satisfaction. The boatman stayed on the boat and took up a long pole. He pushed it over the side and used it to push the craft away from the small landing. The two men who had been helping to load walked off; the boy seemed to have vanished into the evening shadows.

Hal's eyes followed Gilly's pointing finger. 'It's the boatman who brought us to Galat. I wonder if he'd help us?'

'Jouri said the boatmen were different from most Vemorians.'

'Yes, but he'll want paying.'

'He knows Lugh and Jouri have money,' argued Gilly. 'We can say they'll pay him later.'

'It's worth a try,' said Hal.

'It's our only chance,' said Gilly.

'How can we attract his attention?' said Hal. He tried a subdued wave, but the boatman, busy checking his cargo, took no notice. He gave a rope a final tug and took up his pole.

A figure slipped out of the shadows and jumped on to the boat at the other end.

'It's the boy,' said Hal, disappointed. 'Where's the boatman gone? He can't have noticed us.'

Gilly's attention was fixed on the boy. 'Hal,' she whispered. 'That boy. He just came up behind the boatman and thumped him. He's knocked him over.'

'The boy? That's strange, I wonder why?' Hal peered into the gloom. 'He's taken the pole now,' he said.

The boat moved into a pool of light which was

shining on to the canal from a window in one of the
sheds. For the first time, they could see the boy's face.

'Hal,' said Gilly. 'The boy on the boat. It's Bram.'

'What?'

'He's bringing the boat over here.'

'He'll be seen. The Watcher will know he isn't the
boatman.'

'The Watcher is looking the other way,' said Gilly.

At that moment, the Watcher, alerted by the sound
of splashing, turned round. He saw the boat, now half
way across to the bank where Gilly and Hal were. The
Watcher called out to the boat. 'Hey, you down there.
What are you doing?'

'Taking on more cargo for Master Nemgern,' a
voice called back.

'You're right. It is Bram!' said Hal.

'Oh, sssh,' said Gilly. 'Keep quiet, he's nearly here,
we mustn't make the Watcher suspicious.'

'No overloading,' the Watcher called back offi-
ciously.

'No, sir,' Bram replied.

The boat slid into the shadows beside the others.

'Quick,' said Bram's voice. He sounded terrified.
'We must get away, *quickly*.'

They were on board in a flash, hardly noticing the
weight of the head as they swung it on to the boat.
Fortunately, the head was so amazed at being treated
in this desrespectful way that it was momentarily
speechless. At any minute, though, it would protest in
loud and dangerous tones.

'Quick,' said Mab. 'There's an empty barrel here.
Put him in it.'

A moment later, the head was in the barrel with a lid
clapped on top of it. They could hear muffled noises

from within; they hoped desperately that they weren't loud enough to reach the Watcher's ears.

'What have you got back there, next to the raven?' The Watcher's voice carried clearly over the water.

'It's just a barrel of fish,' Mab called back in a placid voice. 'It's mine, I'm taking it up to Herlat to my niece.'

The Watcher grunted, but stayed where he was. Bram manoeuvred the boat out into the canal and they moved slowly away from the bridge.

'Where do you want to go?' said Bram, almost inaudibly.

'Herlat,' said Mab. Bram nodded and began to punt more strongly.

'Where's Herlat?' asked Gilly.

'It's a border town,' said Mab. 'It's the farthest point you can go by water if you want to get to the Walled City. It's a land journey after that.'

Mab ostentatiously wiped her nose with her sleeve. 'Dusty, this boat,' she said in a matter-of-fact way.

Hal had shifted himself along until he was nearer to Bram. 'Bram, are you OK?'

'Yes,' said Bram. 'As OK as anyone can be in this place.'

'Where's the boatman?'

'Lying in the bottom of the boat over there. I think he winded himself when I pushed him over.'

'You're very good at punting,' said Hal after a while.

'I spend a lot of time at school on the river,' said Bram shortly. 'It keeps me fit, and I know about boats and punting and rowing. Some boring school sports do have their uses, you know.'

Hal fell silent again.

'What's in the barrel?' asked Bram, without turning

— 166 —

his head. 'Is it an animal? Can't you keep it quiet? Sound carries a long way over water.'

Hal crawled on his hands and knees to the barrel. He could hear mutterings and mumblings through the cracks.

'This barrel is dirty,' the head was saying. 'This is so great an insult to my god-head that—'

'Shut up,' said Hal through clenched teeth. 'I don't know what you got up to back home that's brought you here, minus your body, but you obviously upset some big cheese in a big way. He didn't order first-class travel for you, so if you aren't exactly comfortable, it's your own fault. I'm not very comfortable either, and nor is Gilly, or Mab. Or Bram, who's saved us all from big trouble. And we haven't done anything at all. So just stow it, will you.'

The head's complaints subsided into a dim mumbling. The water under the flat bottom kept up a steady, even gurgling sound as Bram punted with an easy skill which made Hal envious.

A light shone out from the canalside and swept over the boat. It was so unexpected that Hal and Gilly hardly had time to hurl themselves down on the bottom of the boat. The boat lurched as Bram's pole strokes faltered.

In the bottom of the boat, the boatman stirred.

The light picked out the irregular shape of the cargo, and the voice of a Watcher rang out across the water. 'Badly-packed goods, boatman. Who is the cargo for?'

The Watcher had stopped them beside one of the fine private gardens which ran down to the water's edge, and some people who were walking in the garden came over to see what was going on.

'Trouble, Watcher?' called the voice of a man who was clearly used to ordering people around.

'Nothing important, sir,' the Watcher called back. 'Badly-stowed cargo, I'll search the boat and take a note of the goods, and then make sure the owner of the cargo knows about it. I'll get this boy put to work in the sewers for a few days. That'll teach him.'

'There's more than cargo on that boat.'

The clear voice which rang over the water was all too familiar. 'Search it.'

'Erica!' said Hal.

'What on earth is she doing here, out on the lawn? She's supposed to be a prisoner,' said Gilly. 'A slave.'

'A slave?' said Bram bitterly. 'Erica? You must be joking.'

The boatman sat up with a groan, blinking in the strong light. He rubbed his eyes and shook his head, then got unsteadily to his feet.

'Friend of yours, is she?' he said. 'You're in trouble if she isn't. She's the otherworlder, staying with one of the Twelve, they say.'

'Hold on,' sang out Bram. The boat moved through the water, almost at once out of reach of the light. A hullabaloo broke out behind them; the boatman shoved Bram to one side. He seized the pole and with long, strong strokes, pushed the boat forward at twice the speed.

'Why did you do that?' Gilly asked him in surprise. 'Why didn't you stop and hand us over?'

'Look,' the boatman said. 'I know you're illegals, right? I've been lying there, trying to get my breath back. I can see you're up to no good, and I can tell you're hiding something alive in that barrel of mine.

And I said to myself, this was the lot that Jouri brought to Galat. Well, I say to myself, I can get a bit more than the usual out of Jouri for this. He's a friend, yes, but business is business, and he wouldn't mind paying a bit extra for me to keep my mouth shut about some very fishy goings-on.'

Sweat was pouring down his face. 'Right, so a bit of good business on the quiet is one thing. Messing with one of the Twelve is another. They're no friends of mine. They took my brother away and sent him to work in the stone quarries. I'm not going to help them, not in any way.'

'What will you do?' said Hal.

'Go into hiding,' said the boatman. 'There are ways and means, if you know your way around.'

'We're very grateful,' began Gilly.

'I'm not,' said the boatman brusquely. 'I wish I'd never set eyes on you.'

'Thanks, just the same,' said Hal.

The boatman glared at Bram from under his thick eyebrows. 'And I suppose you'll be wanting to go with your friends here?'

'Yes, he's coming with us,' said Hal firmly.

The boatman brusquely told Bram to sit down, as he was upsetting the balance of the boat. Bram slid down beside the others.

'What's Erica up to?' asked Gilly.

'I can tell you that for nothing,' said Mab. 'She's up to no good.'

Bram agreed. 'When you vanished in the museum, Erica got really cross. She said, "Well, I'll just have to go after them." The next minute, we were walking along a street in Galat. I thought it was another part of the museum, I was just going to say how busy it suddenly was, and why was everybody dressed up like

— 169 —

that, when wham, one of those Watchers grabbed me from behind and I was marched away. Meanwhile, Erica was knocking calmly at the door of some big official-looking building. Someone opened the door and let her in. Then they dragged me off.'

'Didn't she try to help you?'

'No way,' said Bram. 'She never looked round, clearly couldn't care less.'

'And that was the last you saw of her?'

'No, she reappeared that evening. The Watcher had taken me to a place full of other prisoners. They dumped us all into a big room. It was very hot and uncomfortable. Now and again someone who looked like a soldier came and took one of the people in there away. Then, it must have been several hours later, there was a kind of commotion, and Erica appeared. She was with a man and a woman. They were big-wigs, you could tell by the way everyone was bowing and scraping.'

'Did you bow and scrape?'

'No, why should I?' said Bram. 'I was really fed up, so I started shouting at Erica.' He rubbed his cheek. 'Big mistake. She lashed me across the face, and then a soldier dragged me off after them.'

'What for?'

'Questioning,' said Bram. 'Endless questions. All about you, and your family, and my family, and whether you two had ever been through before. I didn't know what they were talking about, and I must have seemed pretty stupid. They whacked me a few times, but I think they realized pretty quickly that there was nothing doing and they dumped me down here to work on the boats. For ever, as far as Erica knows or cares. Cousins!' he added with contempt. 'I've had cousins.'

Hal was looking at Bram with new respect. He seemed much older and stronger than he had back in their world. 'Tough on you,' he said at last.

Bram turned on him. 'Yes, it was, especially since I don't know what they were on about. How much do you know about all this?' He made a sweeping gesture with his hand. 'And just who are these Tuans that Erica was going on about?'

Hal took a deep breath. 'Listen,' he said. 'It's like this.'

Gilly nudged Mab with her foot, carefully, so as not to rock the boat.

Mab didn't want to be disturbed. She was having a beautiful dream. 'I was back in Tuan,' she said with a sigh as she reluctantly woke up. 'Eating chocolate from your world. Heaven.'

'Chocolate,' said Gilly longingly. She didn't want to think about chocolate, it would only make her home-sick.

'Where are the others?' asked Mab, sitting up and yawning.

'Taking turns to help the boatman. I've just done a shift and from what the boatman says, I think we're nearly there. Look, how do we get to the Walled City if we have to go by road?' Gilly went on. 'It's going to be very difficult to carry the head. Is it a long way from the border?'

'Two days' journey,' said Mab. 'And we'll have to travel by night, because although it's Tuan country and there is a treaty, the whole region is under Vemorian control. It'll be crawling with Vemorian spies and spooks and snoops. You can't trust anyone these days.'

Gilly was horrified. 'Two days!'

'Maybe more. It's slower, travelling by night.'

'Mab, what about food? I mean, I'm starving now, although mostly thirsty. But we haven't got any money. We can't walk for miles and miles with nothing to eat.'

'Mmm, I was thinking about that, actually,' said Mab. 'I'm hungry too, that's why I was dreaming about chocolates. I can help . . . perhaps. Once we get across into Tuan lands.'

'How can you help?' Gilly asked doubtfully.

'Maybe there'll be Tuans who will give us food. The Vemorians can't take all the food the country produces. If they won't give us any, why, then we'll take it. And that dratted raven can make itself useful. First cousin to a magpie; it can go and find us some nice shiny coins.'

Gilly didn't like the sound of all this. It seemed very haphazard, and besides, if most of the Tuan food was being taken by the Vemorians, they were probably hungry as well.

'Not as hungry as we are,' said Hal. He was lying low while Bram was punting, keeping a look-out for any pursuing boats.

'They may send someone on by land. To warn the Watchers about us,' Gilly said.

Mab shook her head. 'There aren't the roads,' she said.

'They could signal. Morse code, the Vemorians must have a version of that.'

Again, Mab shook her head. 'I don't think so. They like paper-work. If it isn't written down, they don't believe it. For anything official, you must have a piece of paper.'

'Daft,' said Hal.

'Lucky for us,' said Gilly. 'I don't think we could go any faster. I hope it isn't much further, this is very tiring, and I'm getting thirstier and thirstier.'

'The boatman says about another half hour,' Hal told Gilly after a whispered consultation. 'Here, you take over again, Bram's just about had it. He can rest, and I'll think about what we're going to do when we get across the border.'

'Drink, eat and sleep, I hope,' said Gilly.

'No time for that.' The head's voice was muffled by the barrel. 'We must travel on. My hours will soon be up.'

'What did you say?' asked Hal.

'Nothing,' said the head.

'Nothing, nothing, he said nothing,' repeated the raven, who had been riding along at the front of the boat.

'He means that if the task isn't completed within a certain time, then it can't be done,' said Mab, not sounding very concerned. 'Time runs out on all these things, you know.'

'What do you mean, the task can't be done?'

'If his talking lordship there doesn't get buried within a certain time, then he stays a head,' said Mab.

Gilly stared at her. 'What about Tuan?'

'Tuan will be taken over by the Vemorians.'

'Don't you mind?' said Gilly angrily.

'I mind, but minding won't change anything. What will be, will be.'

'And what about us?' said Gilly.

'I expect you'll stay put.'

'Why didn't he mention this before?' said Gilly furiously. 'How much time have we got?'

'Ask the head.'

The head was now in a huff. 'Never mind,' he said. 'Leave me alone.'

'Do you know?' Gilly asked the raven.

'I do, I do. The head must be buried by the next full moon.'

They all looked up into the clear night sky. 'Is that moon waxing or waning?' asked Gilly. 'It looks full to me now.'

'It's waxing,' said Hal. 'Full tomorrow night, I'd say.'

'What a shame, what a shame, what a shame,' the raven remarked hoarsely.

Gilly sat down with a bump, trying to hold back her tears. 'Then there's no point. There's absolutely nothing we can do. It's impossible for us to get to the Walled City by tomorrow.'

'Come on, Gilly,' said Hal. 'We've got to *think*, not wail.'

'How does thinking help?' said Gilly.

'I don't suppose it does,' said Hal. 'Two into one won't go. Two days' journey, one day to do it in. It can't be done.'

'I'm not giving up,' said Gilly slowly. 'When you put it like that, why can't two into one go? It would be no crazier than the other things that have happened since we came here.'

Mab had been sitting quite still, apparently thinking about chocolate. Now, at Gilly's words she gave a little chirrup of satisfaction.

'Gilly's right,' she said. 'That's the trouble with the younger generation, no faith in the irrational. Hal, give me a map.'

The motion of the boat faltered as Hal considered this extraordinary request. 'I haven't got a map,' he said at last.

'You have,' said Mab. 'No Vemorian boat ever went anywhere without a map. Bram, look in that little locker beside your left foot.'

The boat rocked slightly as Bram did what he was told. Much to Hal's surprise there was indeed a map there. Bram passed it, still folded, down the boat to Mab. She unfolded it, turned it the other way up, then sideways, and then made a satisfied noise.

'Two into one won't go, hey? Wrong. It's difficult to see by moonlight . . . but look at this.'

Bram crawled along the boat to join them, and they looked. 'It's upside down,' Hal said at once.

'No,' said Mab. 'We're here, and that's the border.'

'The writing is upside down,' said Gilly.

'Yes, but it doesn't matter. I have to hold it like this so that I can keep the rights and lefts in order. Look. We're here.' Mab plonked her finger down on the map. 'This is the route to the Walled City.' Her finger followed a twisting, winding brown line.

'Very wriggly road,' said Hal. 'And are those hills? I can see why it takes so much time.'

'Yes,' said Mab. 'Slow. Even slower at night, even with moonlight. And, moreover, that way will be thick with people who want to know where we're going, and why, and what's that you're carrying. No, I've got a much better idea. Now, listen!

'This is my plan . . .'

Nineteen

'PLAN?' SAID GILLY.

'Great,' said Hal.

Mab told them what it was.

'Not so great,' said Hal.

Gilly didn't like the sound of it at all. 'Caves!' she said. 'All that way, underground.' Gilly didn't much like any kind of tunnel, and hated going on the tube when they went to London.

Hal knew how Gilly felt about being in deep, dark places. 'How long will the journey take?' he asked Mab.

'Oh, a few hours,' said Mab vaguely.

Hal was getting suspicious. 'Mab, you're keeping something back. How much do you know about these caves?'

Mab went on the defensive. 'I don't spend my time wandering about underground, do I? What do you take me for? But then I haven't spent much time before now wandering around with a nasty old head that's got to be buried. And, by and large, I think the best Vemorian is one who's a long way away. And here I am, surrounded by them! All right, it was only an idea. You think of a better one.'

'So you haven't ever been in these caves?' Gilly asked.

Mab had to admit that she hadn't. 'Not many

people know about them. They're very, very old; they were dug out in the time of the Old Kings.'

'The same Old Kings that planted that orchard in Vemoria?'

'Yes, Tuan and Vemoria were all one country then. Ruled by the Old Kings.'

Hal was getting interested in the caves. 'So the caves are man-made?'

Mab looked shifty. 'Not exactly *man*-made. Not people . . . not people like us, at any rate.'

'What do you mean?' said Hal, rather brutally. 'Not built by witches, I bet.'

'Witches are people,' said Mab crossly. 'People with special powers.'

'Then who built them? Immortals?'

'I don't know,' said Mab. 'And I don't care, either. They're there, OK? They've always been there. As far as I know, they go right under the mountains. I haven't been through them, but that's what they say.'

Gilly didn't like the sound of this any more than Hal did. 'Caves, witches, underground, the Old Kings . . . it's all too much.'

Bram said nothing.

Mab fell silent, sulking. Hal got to his feet and took over the second punt pole from Bram. Gilly sat with her arms wrapped round her knees, gazing at the reflection of the moon as it shimmered and broke in the water. She looked up at the stars, and thought how much she would like to see the familiar stars of the night sky at home. Not that she ever spent much time looking at them. She left that to Hal with his telescope.

The darkness ahead changed. Little pinpricks of light began to show on the hillside. Then bigger clusters of light. More activity on the water, as the canal widened and became something like a small lake.

The boatman steered the boat towards a landing stage. 'We're here,' he whispered. 'Under cover, all of you.'

Someone hailed them from the stage, asking him who they were, what they were carrying.

'Cargo from Master Nemgern.'

'Carry on.'

'They're quite used to me here,' he explained in a low voice. 'I come up with goods quite often. I don't think they'll bother with me. You should be able to get ashore without anyone taking any notice, and I'm going to do my vanishing act. Tell Jouri he owes me.'

He was right. Master Nemgern was either too mean or too unimportant to land his cargoes at any of the main landing places, which were well lit. Even at this time of night, they were busy, with far too many Vemorians strolling about.

Mab was off first. 'This way,' she said, vanishing into the dark cover of a wall. 'This half of the town belongs to Vemoria. We need to get across to the old part, there will be Tuans there who can help us.'

They crept up a dark alleyway. There was some kind of disturbance happening on the quay beneath them. A good thing, thought Gilly. Surely nobody would notice them with a fuss going on down there.

'Some nob arriving,' said Hal. 'We've been lucky.'

It was as well they couldn't see the vessel that had come in to land just after theirs. This was no barge, no flat-bottomed punt. This was a fast ship, a thing of beauty in its lines, which told of power and speed. The standard of the Twelve flapped at its prow. A dozen tired men rested on their oars, as a tall man in a dark cloak came down the gangplank, followed by another man, equally tall, and the shorter figure of a girl.

The people around whispered, then fell silent. They couldn't remember ever seeing one of the Twelve there before. Together with that other man; low voices whispered that he was the Chief Warden. And the girl, a stranger by the look of her, an otherworlder. What was she doing here, in that company?

The four of them should have moved faster than they ever had in their lives, but they were tired and hungry and unsuspecting of what Erica might be planning. So they plodded on, thinking only of how much they wanted something to eat and drink.

'I have a friend here,' said Mab. 'She lives just a few streets away. She'll take us in, and help us on our way.'

'Sssh,' said Gilly, stopping abruptly.

'Come on, Gilly,' said Hal in a weary voice.

'Listen.'

'I can't hear anything.'

'A donkey,' said Gilly. 'I can hear a donkey.'

'So what? If the canal stops here, I expect they have dozens of donkeys. You don't imagine they catch a Number seventy-two bus up to the next town, do you?'

'Not any donkey,' said Gilly. 'It's Lugh's donkey.'

'Rubbish.'

Mab listened, holding up a warning hand. 'Gilly is right, that braying sounds very familiar.'

'It's getting close,' said Gilly. 'It's somewhere round that corner.'

With that she darted off, followed by Bram, leaving an exasperated Hal standing in the roadway with Mab and the head, who was starting to make some very unenthusiastic noises. The raven was jumping up and down, abusing Gilly. 'Don't be silly, don't be silly.'

Mab set off after Gilly and Bram. Hal had no idea where they were going, and so, he thought furiously, I just have to wait here like a lemon.

Voices. Greetings. Laughter.

Hope rose, then faded. No, thought Hal. They couldn't possibly be here.

They were.

Lugh, Jouri and the two donkeys came clattering round the corner where Gilly had gone. They were talking, laughing, asking questions.

'I knew you would come here,' said Lugh, his eyes shining with excitement. 'I could see it in my head, quite clearly. Not how you would get here, or when, but just that you would. So we just headed for here, and hoped that you would somehow find your way. And you did.'

Jouri turned to Bram. 'And who is this?' he asked.

'Bram,' said Hal. 'Our cousin.'

'And the other one?' Jouri looked suddenly serious. 'What about her?'

Gilly pulled a face. 'Bad news. She's thrown in her lot with the Vemorians, it seems.'

Lugh's face was serious now. 'Have you got the head? They didn't get the head, did they?'

'It's here,' said Hal.

Lugh clasped his arm and let out a sigh of relief. 'Then we still have a chance. It's a tricky journey from here to the Walled City, but nothing compared to what we've come through. We can do it.'

Hal hated to dash his hopes. 'It isn't so easy,' he began, but Jouri interrupted.

'We mustn't stand and talk here,' he said. 'This may be Tuan, but it isn't safe, not these days. We need to be inside, behind locked doors and shuttered windows before we talk.'

Mab had been flitting up and down in her excitable way. Now she waved a hand grandly down the street. 'My old friend Zenobia lives near here. She will welcome us, I know.'

'Zenobia!' said Jouri.

'Yes, Zenobia,' said Mab, taken aback at the tone of Jouri's voice. 'An old friend, from my childhood.'

'And in the power of the Vemorians,' said Jouri grimly. 'She'll betray us all as soon as look at us.'

'You're crazy,' said Mab. 'Zenobia? I'd trust her with my life.'

'Then you would be very stupid,' said Jouri. 'Her husband and children have been taken away to Vemoria as hostages. She'd do anything to get them back, and betraying all of us would do her good with the Vemorians.'

Mab understood now. 'Zenobia, too?' she commented sadly.

'That's blown it, then,' said Hal impatiently. 'What do we do now?'

'No problem,' said Jouri. 'My nephew lives here.'

'How do we know he isn't being held over a barrel by the big Vs?' asked Gilly. 'The same as this Zenobia person?'

Mab shook her head. 'It's not the same,' she said. 'Friendship, yes, it's a tie. But family . . . It's difficult to explain. Family comes first. Always. In whatever circumstances. Jouri's nephew has to help him.'

Jouri's nephew turned out to be about the same age as Jouri, and very like him.

'My oldest brother was much older than me,' Jouri explained. 'He was grown up and married by the time I was born. So Delert here is older than me.'

Food was scarce in this part of Tuan, Delert told them, apologizing for what he said was very plain fare. Hal and Gilly couldn't imagine what he normally ate if he felt this was plain.

As they wolfed the fresh bread, spread with thick butter and hunks of unfamiliar but very tasty cheese, Gilly and Hal heard how Lugh and Jouri had been with Wylith when the Wardens came. Wylith had realized that somehow the Vemorians had broken through the spells which the white-haired man used to keep strangers away from the main part of his house, and had led them quickly away to another house.

'We didn't know what had happened to you, so we thought it best to stay there,' said Lugh. 'We reckoned that the Wardens were looking for us, and for the head in particular, and we were sure they must have caught you.'

Jouri took up the story. 'Later on, Wylith came back. He had been doing a bit of scouting, wanting to know what they had done with his master. He gathered from hearing a couple of junior Wardens talking that they had put his master in prison, but it was clear that they hadn't got you or the head.'

'It would have been the worse for them if they had laid their corrupt hands on me,' proclaimed the head, who was sitting in a corner, still wrapped in his tarpaulin.

Bram looked uneasily towards the head. He'd only caught a glimpse of it, but it had given him the heebie-jeebies. He hoped the others weren't about to uncover it and bring it out.

The others took no notice. 'The donkeys had been taken to this same house earlier,' Jouri went on, 'so for everyone's sake, we thought we'd better make ourselves scarce. We found a boat, and here we are.'

'I'm so glad,' said Gilly. 'It sounds as if we have a difficult journey ahead, and we wouldn't want to do it without you.'

'It shouldn't be too bad,' said Delert. 'It's two or three days' ride, if you keep up a fair pace. Nothing excessive; that might attract attention.'

'We can't go that way,' said Hal.

Lugh, Jouri and Delert looked at him in surprise.

'There is no other way,' said Delert. 'Why can't you go that way?'

'The head has to be buried before the next full moon,' said Gilly glumly.

Lugh stared at her. 'But that's tomorrow. Where do you get this idea from?'

Hal jerked his head in the direction of the tarpaulin. 'He told us. Just like that. So Mab says that our only chance is to take another route, through some caves, an underground way she knows about.'

Silence.

Jouri shook his head in disbelief. 'The Caves? The Caves of the Unspoken Ones? It's impossible.'

Delert puffed out his cheeks and made blowing noises of disapproval, po, po, po.

'Jouri's right. That's not the way to go.'

'Is there a way through these caves – what did you call them? The Caves of the Unspoken Ones? Like Mab said?' Hal asked.

'I'm not saying there *isn't* such a way,' said Delert

cautiously. 'I'm just saying that it's no way for you to go.'

'Is it dangerous?' asked Gilly. 'Do you need to be an expert pot-holer or something?'

'Dangerous? Dangerous isn't the word,' said Jouri. 'No, it's out of the question. I couldn't let you do it.'

'We have to,' said Hal. 'Why can't any of you say what the problem is? What are these caves like?'

Mab looked at Jouri and Delert, and then looked up at the ceiling. Jouri and Delert looked at each other, and said nothing.

Hal turned to Lugh. 'Are you going to tell us? What's the matter? Is it a quicker way? Is it worse than the swamp or the Wild Forest? Are we going to get lost again?'

Lugh lifted his hands in a gesture of defeat.

'I don't know,' he said finally.

'Don't know if we'll get lost?' said Gilly. 'Of course you don't. But is it likely? Are these caves the kind of place where you do get lost?'

'I don't know,' said Lugh again. 'I've never been in them.'

'Jouri, Delert? Come on, what are they like? Mab, do you know?'

'Er, no, not exactly,' said Mab.

'None of us knows,' said Lugh. 'You see, we can't go into them. No Tuan can.'

'Why on earth not?' said Hal.

The head spoke from his corner. 'It is forbidden,' he said. 'The Caves of the Unspoken Ones are the realm of the Unspoken Ones. It is territory forbidden to Tuans and to Vemorians. None of them may pass the entrance. They guard the gateways, but may never pass through them.'

'Who says?' Hal was unimpressed.

'It has always been so,' said the head.

'Very helpful,' muttered Hal.

Gilly was thinking. 'You aren't a Tuan or a Vemorian, are you?' she said to the head.

The raven, who had been enjoying a quiet snooze, opened one sharp eye. 'Don't be ridiculous, don't be ridiculous. The god-head is an Immortal. The petty customs and ways of Tuans and Vemorians are nothing to him, nothing at all.'

'Fine,' said Gilly. 'In that case, *we* can go into these caves, Hal and Bram and I, and we can take cutesie-pie here with us. I suppose you'll have to come, too,' she added for the benefit of the raven. 'Can't see you not being around to stick your nasty sharp beak into whatever's going on.'

Lugh, Jouri and Delert all spoke at once.

'Impossible!'

'Out of the question!'

'You'll never make it.'

Hal noticed that Lugh's concern was still more for the success of their mission than for his and Gilly's safety. This annoyed him.

'I think it's worth a try, don't you, Gilly?'

'You'll go anyway, won't you?' she said shrewdly. 'So I don't suppose I've got much choice.'

'Bram?'

Bram got up and moved away from the others. 'I can't,' he said in an uneven voice. 'I can't go into caves.'

'What do you mean, you can't go into caves?' said Hal. 'I thought you were the great sporty one.'

'No caves,' said Bram.

Gilly looked at him. 'Is it a phobia, Bram?'

He nodded.

'Well, I think Bram's been very brave, and we

— 185 —

wouldn't have got this far without his help. So what does it matter if he can't come through the caves with us?'

'He can travel with us, over the mountains,' said Jouri.

Mab was shaking her head in a doleful way. 'I should never have mentioned the Caves, I should have kept my mouth shut.'

Lugh's eyes were fixed on Hal and Gilly. 'No, Aunt, you did the right thing,' he said. 'It's up to these two, then. It's their decision, and our only hope.'

Hal looked at Lugh. 'Any of your powers returning? Can you tell us whether we'll make it through the caves? And in time to bury the head?'

Lugh shook his head. 'I can tell you nothing, it's beyond any powers I have. Mab's still got some of her magic because witches are different from other Tuans. They are born as witches, with all their powers. What there is of them,' he added unkindly. 'It isn't the same magic as the rest of us Tuans have.'

'What are you going to do, all you Tuans, if you get your magic back?' asked Gilly.

'Does it matter?' Lugh was flushed. 'You won't be here, you'll be back in your own world.'

Gilly said nothing.

Jouri gave a slight cough. 'All the Tuans want is their land and their own way of life back. To live the way we and our families have for generations, with the Vemorians away on the other side of a distant border.'

'Can you do that?' asked Gilly doubtfully. 'Can you ever go back and have things the way they were before? It's not like that in our world.'

'Our world isn't the same as yours,' said Lugh. 'Of course everything can be the same as it was.'

The head laughed, a mirthless, sinister laugh.

'These earth dwellers may be better at foreseeing the future than you are, Tuan soothsayer,' he said mockingly. 'Vemoria has changed, and that has changed the lives of the Tuans.'

'It's not important.' Lugh glanced at Delert and Jouri. 'If they're going, they should start. Time is short.'

Jouri got up from the table. 'We don't know if they are going,' he said.

'Yes, they are, yes, they are,' croaked the raven. 'Come along, come along, no time to lose. What a shame, what a shame, what a shame.'

'What a pain, what a pain, what a pain,' said Gilly to Hal. He choked back a laugh. 'No time for jokes.'

'Always time for jokes,' said Jouri. 'Gilly and Hal, Bram will travel with us. If you get through the Caves, wait for him on the hill beyond the Walled City.' He became practical, his voice brisker. 'Now, how are you going to carry the head? If we put it back in the barrel it's going to be very heavy and unwieldy.'

'The donkey can go,' said Mab.

The others stared at her. 'Can it?' said Lugh. 'Are you sure?'

'It isn't a Tuan or a Vemorian, it's just a donkey. Animals can go into the caves.'

'I'm going,' said the raven self-importantly. 'Although I am, of course, a sacred bird.'

'Perhaps it's a sacred donkey,' said Hal. 'It's worth a try. What happens if Mab is wrong? Does the donkey turn to stone, or become rooted to the spot, or what?'

'You'll know, because if it can pass through the gateway, then it can go with you. There is a barrier of ancient and very strong magic, not Tuan magic, something quite else. That's what stops us. It shouldn't stop you, or the head, or the donkey.'

'Or me, or me.'

Screech, screech, thought Gilly. I can just imagine what you're going to sound like, echoing round these caves.

Mab got up. 'There's one thing you must remember when you go through the Caves.'

They waited.

'Nothing,' said Mab, 'is what it seems.'

Twenty

'THE GATEWAY,' SAID DELERT.

He was clearly not at all happy. He had pushed aside a solid-looking oak cupboard, revealing nothing but a black space. Not a gloomy space, or a hole in the wall, but a patch of darkness so black that you felt you could drown in it.

'Oh,' said Gilly at last. 'Is that it?'

'Creepy,' said Hal. 'But at least it doesn't seem to be worrying the donkey. I mean, animals have a sixth sense about danger . . . things that are wrong. Don't they?'

'Possibly,' said Gilly, who privately thought that this donkey was a very dim specimen, which would hardly make it into the two-sense league.

Certainly the donkey, laden with the head in a canvas bag on one side and two stout spades on the other, looked very placid and unconcerned.

'How do we go through?' Gilly asked Delert.

Hal took the donkey's bridle from Lugh and braced himself.

'You just, well, walk through,' said Delert. 'If I tried, it would be like trying to walk through a brick wall. Watch!'

To prove his point, Delert went up to the black panel, and tried to keep walking. Gilly winced as he clonked against what was obviously solid wall.

He retreated, rubbing his nose and arms.

'You try.'

Gilly advanced carefully, her right arm out in front of her. She fully expected the same to happen to her; instead, her right arm simply disappeared. She stretched out the other one, and that, too, became invisible in the melting blackness.

'Here goes,' she said. 'See you on the other side.' Taking a deep breath, she walked forward, and vanished.

Hal plunged after her, dragging the donkey behind him, ignoring the curses and protests from the head and raven. There was panic in his voice as he, too, was lost in the black patch, his shouts of 'Gilly, wait! Wait for me, wait!' cut off abruptly as he passed through the wall.

Gilly stood stock still, blinking. It wasn't dark, but the light was very strange. It was like looking through a blue filter. Dark, purplish blue, not a bright, summer's day blue.

She could hear Hal calling, first as though from a long way away, and then closer. She could hear a snuffling sound, and the click of little hooves on the stone floor, but she couldn't see Hal or the donkey. She looked harder into the blue gloom, and let out a yelp.

No Hal. No donkey. No spades or carrier. There was only the head, suspended in mid-air, glowing with a blue haze. Even his eyeballs were blue.

'Gilly! GILLY!'

Her name rang round the stone walls and came back to her over and over, fading away into a chilly whimper . . . G i l l y.

'Hal, I'm here. Where are you? Where's the donk? What's happened to the head?'

Gilly's voice was almost in Hal's ear. He swung his arm round in an arc.

'Ow! Something swiped at me.'

'It's me,' said Hal.

'No, it isn't,' said Gilly. 'I can't see you anywhere.'

'I can't see you, but I'm right next to you.'

Gilly did a swing of her own. 'You're right. And I can't see you.' Gilly was seriously puzzled. She could see herself, but not Hal. 'Can you see yourself, Hal?'

'Yes,' came back an echoing whisper. 'And I can see the head.'

'I don't like this one bit,' said Gilly.

'No,' agreed Hal. 'It's spooky.'

Their eyes were getting used to the strange light, and they were able to take in more of their surroundings. Enormous boulders were flung around in an immense cavern of rock. The walls were rough and formed in grotesque shapes. Only the ground was smooth.

'It looks as though it's been polished,' said Gilly. 'The stone floor. It's very slippery, too,' she added, as she slid a foot along it.

'It's going to be tricky, walking on it,' said Hal.

'How do we know which way we should go?' said Gilly, looking at the huge spaces all around them.

The raven had been exploring. The flapping of her wings was bad enough as it echoed eerily back at them. Now it cawed, and Hal and Gilly nearly jumped out of their skins as a thousand caws and croaks came at their ears from every side, rattling round their heads until the horrible sound finally died away.

'Don't do that,' said Gilly. 'Just don't do that.'

The raven tried to speak softly, and came out with a strange, rasping noise.

—— 191 ——

'Sounds like you did when you had bronchitis,' Hal observed.

'I will lead the way,' grated the invisible bird.

'Thanks a lot,' said Hal. 'You do that. Just one little problem, don't let it bother you.'

'Caw?'

'We can't see you, you idiotic bird.'

'Caw. What a shame, what a shame, what a shame.'

Gilly was shivering. 'It isn't exactly cold,' she explained, her teeth chattering, 'but it still makes me shiver.'

Hal found the sound of invisible teeth chattering distinctly alarming. Gilly was right. The cavern they were in wasn't cold in terms of temperature, but there was an innate coldness to it. Hal had sometimes felt that kind of coldness when he looked at stars, so unimaginably far away, and felt himself to be nothing but a speck of dust dancing on the surface of a star.

'Indifference,' he said. 'Nothing here cares about us, or the head. Or the Tuans and Vemorians, for that matter.'

'I know what you mean,' said Gilly. 'And I don't like it. Hal, we must start. This floor is horrible to walk on. It may not be far as the crow – or raven – flies, but it's going to be slow.'

Hal looked round, trying to get his bearings in the eerie blue light.

'Are you holding the donkey?' Gilly's voice sounded as though it was behind him now.

'Yes.'

'And the head's still in a bag lashed to the donkey's saddle?'

'Yes.'

'Then you set off, and I'll follow the head. As long as he glows, I can see where you are.'

— 192 —

'That might work,' said Hal. 'You'll have to keep talking, though, so I know you're still following us.'

'I will,' said Gilly. 'By the way, the head's strangely silent.'

They both looked at the head.

'I think he's having a fit,' said Hal with interest.

'He does seem upset,' said Gilly. 'Why doesn't he tell us what's the matter?'

'I don't think he can,' said Hal. 'His mouth's moving, as though he's saying something, but there's no sound.'

'The god-head can be seen but not heard, seen but not heard,' croaked the raven.

'And we can be heard but not seen. What a place,' said Gilly with feeling. 'Still, we can do without bossyboots going on at us. Come on, Hal, the sooner we get moving, the sooner we'll be out of here.'

Hal turned round in a complete circle. One area of the huge cave seemed darker than the rest. Perhaps that was the way to go. He was beginning to feel hopeless about the whole business, but he didn't want to tell Gilly that.

'Into the darkness,' said Gilly's voice. 'It's solid walls everywhere else. If there's a way through, it must be down there.'

Sliding and slipping, moving at a snail's pace, they eased their way towards the darkness. Hal, trying to go faster, fell several times, until Gilly, angry with fear, yelled at him to slow down.

'If you let go of the donkey and it careers off, we're done for.'

'Done for, done for, done for, done for,' came echoing back in wrap-around stereo sound.

'This is hopeless,' said Hal.

'Hopeless, hopeless, hopelessss.'

'Shut UP!'

'Up, up up up ppppp.'

And then, 'It isn't so blue any more,' said Gilly with relief.

It was true. The heavy blue light, which had been so dispiriting, was giving way to a lighter grey. The air which had smelt, Gilly thought, like a dry cleaners', became fresher. Gilly was trying not to think about failure, not to allow herself to despair. Concentrate, she told herself. Think of summer, of clear streams and mountain air and warm sun.

They edged round a boulder which towered above them, way up into the gloom. Gilly stopped. 'I don't believe it,' she breathed.

As quickly as a cut from one scene to another in a film, everything had changed. They were in a valley, set about with thick trees. Grassy banks led down to just such a stream as she had been thinking of. She could hear birds, the burbling of the stream, the sound of distant bells.

Heaven, thought Gilly. An easy path wound down to the stream, and then stretched out invitingly before them. Gilly could see the head in front, no longer blue, but more his normal greeny tones.

Unfortunately, she still couldn't see Hal or the raven or the donkey, but it didn't matter. For the first time, she felt they really might get to the Walled City in time.

Hal was coughing.

'What's the matter?' asked Gilly.

'This awful fog,' said Hal miserably. 'I was just thinking about that day last winter when I went to school in thick fog and nearly knocked old Mrs Grosbank over. When it was so cold and wet and beastly, and you got bronchitis and were off school for two weeks. And here we are, in the thick of it, can't see a step in front of me, freezing cold. However are we going to find our way?'

'What are you talking about?' said Gilly. Had Hal gone mad? 'Fog?' she said. 'There isn't any fog. It's beautiful sunshine, and I can see the path as clearly as anything.'

'Don't be stupid,' said Hal. 'You remind me of that awful friend of Mum's who used to tell us that you feel better at once if you smile.'

'Well, you do,' said Gilly. 'This is ridiculous. I'm right next to you, and I'm in a wonderful, warm, sunlit valley, and you're floundering around in wintry fog.'

'Raven,' said Hal. 'Where are you? What can you see?'

'Great black crags,' said the raven with huge satisfaction. 'And fields full of things for me to eat.'

'OK,' said Gilly. 'I don't think we want to know. Hal, the head's trying to tell us something.'

The head might have been, but his rolling eyes, look of fury and silent mouthings didn't leave them any the wiser.

'Nothing is what it seems,' Gilly said to herself. 'I wonder.' She shut her eyes, and, just for a moment, remembered the November days that Hal had been talking about. When she opened her eyes again, there was the fog. She felt the chill beginning to freeze her hands and nose.

At once she shut her eyes, desperately imagining the warm, summer, mountain scene. Thank goodness. The fog had gone, the picture postcard view was back.

'Hal, you see what you're thinking about,' she said urgently. 'Shut your eyes and see what I'm seeing. Like we do when we want to try out telepathy. Think

—— 195 ——

about the summer, and mountains, and a bubbling stream. Please, Hal.'

It worked.

Hal grudgingly, unconvinced, shut his eyes, and found a scene very like the one Gilly described taking shape in his mind. When he opened his eyes again, there it was, just as Gilly had said.

It was the strangest journey that could be imagined. There was no physical effort, the path was easy – as long as they kept a picture of a gentle walk through pleasant countryside in their minds. But anything they thought about, they saw.

It was disconcerting when a pizza parlour sprang up in front of Hal's eyes. Twice, Gilly found herself heading for her school gates. Then she was in a traffic jam on the motorway, feeling sick with the fumes and heat on a sticky summer outing. Once it was Christmas, with shops full of decorations.

Then there were grimmer places, dredged up from nightmares. Sandy wastes, littered with distorted, writhing creatures. Slimy, crumbling steps leading down into terrible dungeons in the bowels of the earth.

The further they went, the harder it was to concentrate, to keep the vision of an easy, pleasant way in their minds; the more they felt compelled, against their wills, to create appalling, desolate landscapes.

'Think sun,' said Gilly desperately.

'And green.'

'Remember that beck behind our cottage that summer we went to the Lakes?'

'Travel brochures for Switzerland,' said Hal.

'I can't go on,' said Gilly.

'We have to,' said Hal.

The raven had been unusually silent, no doubt travelling along thinking with pleasure about things that would give anybody else the creeps. Now she burst into a loud caw.

'Danger, danger. I hear danger. We are being pursued, yes, pursued.'

Hal and Gilly stopped, closed their eyes and listened. There was a distant, very faint sound. A mixture of howling and barking. And a voice, a voice from their world, just audible, urging the barking creatures on, like a huntsman with a pack of hounds . . .

'Erica,' said Hal.

'With hounds,' said Gilly.

'The hunting dogs of Vemoria,' said the raven. 'Famous for their speed, tenacity and for always getting their prey. Half dog, half wolf, they say. Yes, half wolf. What a shame, what a shame, what a shame.'

'What do they hunt?' asked Gilly.

'As if we didn't know,' said Hal.

'People,' said the raven. 'People.'

Twenty-One

'WE CAN REASON WITH ERICA,' SAID HAL.
Hal listened to the howls of the hounds, getting distinctly closer. 'I think not,' he said.

The donkey seemed to be getting restless, judging by the shuffling noises it was making and the way the head was bouncing up and down.

'Of course, we can just hide, she probably can't see us.'

'No, but those dogs can smell us, and besides, I bet it's the head she's after. She's been brainwashed by the Vemorians.'

'They wouldn't need to brainwash her, she's got a head full of bad ideas to start with.'

'They're getting nearer.'

'Run.'

They ran, pulling the donkey behind them. The mountain landscape had vanished. So had the fog and the nightmares. They were back in blue caves again, very dry this time, with strange blue sand at their feet.

'Beastly to run through,' panted Gilly.

'And I don't think we're getting anywhere useful,' said Hal.

They skidded through a narrow passage between two outcrops of jagged blue rocks and came to an abrupt halt. There in front of them was a cliff face of stone. It was smooth, dark and filled the end of the cave. It seemed to be part of the rocks on either side. There was no way round it, and certainly no question of climbing it.

'Even if we could, what about the donkey?' said Hal.

As the hounds came closer, the echoes got louder and louder. It sounded as though thousands of wild animals were loose in the caves. Gilly knew she was white with fear; at least Hal couldn't see her. It wouldn't have mattered, because Hal wasn't very keen on the situation either.

'Quick. Back the way we came,' said Gilly. 'There must be another way out.'

'The hounds are into that last cave,' said Hal. He looked up at the sheer stone face in front of them.

'There's writing on it,' said Gilly.

'Where?' said Hal, peering up into the gloom.

Etched in deep letters was KILROY WAS HERE.

'What?'

'Kilroy was here . . .'

The hounds were pouring into the passageway between the two caves.

'It's not real,' Gilly shrieked. 'The wall isn't real. Go through it, go through.'

She lunged for the head, found the donkey's halter, and pulled the animal towards the wall. Hal on the other side of the donkey, was pulling the other way, telling her to stop, 'You're crazy . . .'

The stone wall evaporated before their eyes. They were in darkness again, but a familiar, everday, above-ground darkness. As her eyes adjusted, Gilly began to see the outline of the donkey . . . and Hal.

He was grinning all over his face. 'Clever Gilly.'

'It was the same as earlier on. You remember what Mab said to us? "Nothing is what it seems?" That went for the stone cliff, as well.'

They could no longer hear the hounds or Erica's shrill, vengeful voice.

'She'll be stuck there for a good long time, I hope,' said Hal with satisfaction. 'It'll never occur to her that a stone wall two hundred feet high only exists in her mind.'

Gilly was taking in their new surroundings. In the distance she could see a glimmer of light. A sloping path led towards it.

'I think we're in a real cave, Hal,' she said. 'It smells normal, and it looks like any other cave. I think we've come through.'

'I hope you're right,' said Hal, giving the donkey a friendly shove to set her off on the path.

The glimmer of light got bigger as they got nearer to it, until they could see that it was an opening out of the cave. Hal went first and peered through.

'Yes!' He leapt for joy, and punched the lovely, clear, moonlit air. 'No more caves, just open country-side.'

Gilly joined him, as the donkey clattered up the slope behind them. She threw herself down on the grass and looked up at the sky, still light over to the west, and with the first few stars showing.

The raven broke the silence.

'No time to lose, no time to lose. The moon is up, yes, up.'

Gilly sat up abruptly. She and Hal looked to the horizon where, out of a thin drift of sunset clouds, a huge, glowing moon was rising.

'Full moon,' said Hal. 'Now what do we do?'

'Ask the head, he'll tell us.'

They pulled the barrel off the donkey's saddle, and

lifted the head out. Then they put it carefully on the ground and looked at it, waiting for it to boom out at them in its usual way.

'He looks bad,' said Hal.

The raven flapped anxiously round, cawing to the head to open his great eyes. The eyelids fluttered slightly, and then . . . nothing.

The head clearly wasn't going to tell them anything.

'Hal, you don't think he's dead?' Gilly sounded as alarmed as she felt.

'Doesn't look very alive,' said Hal, 'but then he should have been dead days ago.'

The head's blue pallor had gone, and his face was looking grey. The bedraggled locks hung over his great forehead.

'He isn't bleeding any more,' Gilly pointed out.

'No time to waste, no time to waste,' shrieked the raven. 'Bury him, bury him.'

'We'd better,' said Hal. 'I just hope it isn't too late.'

'It can't be,' said Gilly, who was fighting back her tears. 'Quick, get the spades.'

'Where do we bury him?' said Hal, looking around in despair.

'Oh, anywhere,' said Gilly. 'What does it matter?'

'I'm trying to remember exactly what Lugh told us . . . it seems so long ago.'

'On a hill,' said Gilly.

'There are hills all around,' said Hal.

'Look,' said Gilly. 'Up there, on the top.' She pointed towards some shadowy shapes which were just visible in the twilight. 'There's a kind of circle of stones.'

'That's it,' said Hal. 'We'll bury him there.'

The moon had now risen well above the horizon. Gilly and Hal snatched a spade each and leaving the head under the care of the distressed but watchful raven, they ran up the few yards to the top of the hill.

It was completely still inside the circle of stones. The breeze had dropped, and there were none of the usual night sounds, no rustling, no animal sounds, nothing.

'Magic,' said Gilly in a whisper.

'This is the centre,' said Hal, who had paced it out. 'We'll dig here.'

Digging holes is hard work. Gilly often helped her mother in the garden, but a hole for a rose was a doddle in comparison to this. The ground was hard and dry, and as fast as they shovelled up the earth, it ran back down into the hole.

'Dump the earth further away from the hole,' suggested Gilly.

'The sides are going to cave in before it's big enough to hold the head,' said Hal.

'Shouldn't we bury it six feet under?' said Gilly helpfully.

'I hope you're joking,' said Hal, who was getting hotter and hotter and more and more red in the face.

'That will just have to do,' he said.

Gilly pushed back another landslip of earth which had tumbled back into the hole.

'I'll stop it from collapsing while you get the head,' she panted. 'Quickly, look how high the moon is.'

Hal slid back down the hill, and picked up the head. It felt heavy and lifeless, and very unpleasant. I'm off decapitation, thought Hal as he struggled up to the top.

Gilly thrust the spades to one side, and watched as Hal lowered the head into the hole.

'Only just big enough,' she said. She picked up a

spade, and began to pack the earth back in round the head. Some tears splashed on to the earth as she piled it up. 'Goodbye, head,' she said sadly.

'What are you crying for?' said Hal, who was feeling a bit tearful himself, but didn't want to admit it. 'He was very nasty.'

'I know, but we've made a long journey together. And I think we're too late. And I'm so tired.'

She felt in her pocket for her handkerchief, and as she pulled it out, some black specks fell to the ground.

'You've dropped something,' said Hal, patting down the final layer of earth on the head. He didn't like to stamp it down, it seemed unfeeling, so he left it heaped up in a mound.

Gilly investigated. 'They look like apple seeds,' she said. 'I don't know how they got there.'

'Big apple,' said Hal, yawning. 'Look at the size of them.'

'Mmm,' said Gilly sleepily.

The donkey was waiting where they had left it, pulling up mouthfuls of thick grass and chomping contentedly.

'Now what?' said Hal.

'Let's just lie down for a bit,' said Gilly. 'I'm so tired.'

'What if Erica and those hounds come rushing out of the cave?'

'What cave?' said Gilly. 'There is no cave, now.'

She was right. Where the entrance to the cave had been, there was now a grassy hillock, with some rocks dotted about on it.

'There's very strong magic here,' said Gilly. 'And I don't think I can stay awake another minute.'

'What about the raven?' said Hal, sinking to the ground beside Gilly.

'She's guarding the head,' said Gilly.

And out of the shadows of the stone circle they could hear, 'What a shame, what a shame, what a shame.'

They slept.

Twenty-Two

'WAKE UP!'

Someone was calling Gilly. She was soundly asleep; was it really time to get up? It felt like the middle of the night.

Then she remembered where she was. Bemused, she sat up, stretching and yawning, and rubbing her eyes.

Hal, with all his old skill at sleeping through anything, didn't stir.

'Erugh?' said Gilly, her eyes still heavy with sleep. Who was standing there, waiting for her to wake up? A familiar figure . . .

It was Lugh. And beside him stood the wary figure of Bram. When he saw Gilly wake up, a huge, relieved smile spread across his face.

It all came flooding back. The journey through the caves, burying the head . . .

Gilly got up, feeling thick-headed and dim-witted. Best to come straight out with it. 'I'm sorry, Lugh,' she said. 'We didn't get here in time.'

'Are you sure?' said Lugh. 'All kinds of strange things have happened. There's been a tremendous thunderstorm, and the canal from Galat to Herlat has been washed away. And look. That's always been bare hillside, I remember coming here when I was little.' He pointed up to the top of the hill.

Gilly blinked. There was no stone circle on the top of the hill. Instead there was a grove of fully grown trees, looking as though they had been there for a hundred years.

Gilly shook Hal out of his sleep, and pushed and bullied him to his feet, exclaiming and pointing up the hill.

'What are you on about?' He spotted Lugh. 'Hi, Lugh. And Bram. How did you get here?' Then he saw where Gilly was pointing. Suddenly he was wide awake.

They ran up the slope. The stones were still there, but they lay on their sides, overgrown with moss. Hal jabbed at one with his toe. 'Embedded in the earth,' he said. 'They look as though they've been there for centuries.'

Gilly took no notice. She was staring at the centre of the ring of trees where she expected to see the heaped mound of earth.

No mound. Instead, a huge, ancient apple tree was growing there.

'With leaves and blossom and apples all at the same time,' Gilly said wonderingly.

'Where did you bury the head?' Lugh had followed them up to the top.

Gilly pointed. 'Where the apple tree is. Only it was all bare, then. No trees, and the stones standing in a circle.'

'We couldn't have got here in time,' said Gilly again. 'We were too late. The head had died.'

'The Fountain, the Sacred Fountain in the centre of the Walled City is flowing once more,' said Lugh. 'That must mean something.'

Hal's face lit up. 'Were we in time, then? But how did all these trees get here?'

'Magic,' said Gilly. She looked out to where they could see the higgledy-piggledy streets of the Walled City laid out like a map, down below them.

'Where are the others?' she asked Lugh. 'And how did you get here so quickly?'

'Quickly?' said Lugh, astonished. 'It was a terrible journey. Slow, and difficult. And then, with the storm . . .'

Hal was looking puzzled. 'Gilly,' he said. 'It was evening when we fell asleep, and it's evening now. Look at the long shadows.'

'You're right,' said Gilly. 'And, oh, Hal! Look at the moon.'

The moon was rising above the horizon once more, not such a huge and vibrant moon this time, and no longer full.

'How long have we slept?' said Hal.

Gilly looked surprised. 'Twenty-four hours, I suppose.'

Hal was thinking. 'More like three days,' he said, 'judging by the moon.' Those hours peering through his telescope hadn't been wasted.

'We left Herlat three days ago,' said Lugh.

'It wasn't an ordinary sleep, then,' said Hal.

'Probably not,' said Lugh.

Gilly suddenly remembered Erica. 'Hal! What about Erica? Do you think she's still in the caves?'

'I hope so,' said Hal. 'I hope those hounds have eaten her for breakfast.'

'Hal!'

'She's a pain,' said Hal. 'It's a shame, I didn't think anybody could be like that, but she's ghastly, and she's been horrible. She didn't need to side with the Vemorians like that.'

'She's one of them,' said Bram firmly.

— 207 —

'What a shame!' said Gilly, remembering something else. Her eyes searched the surrounding landscape, which was now bathed in gentle moonlight. 'Where's the raven?'

'Caw.'

With a great beating of wings, the raven landed at their feet. 'Here I am, off you go, off you go. The godhead no longer needs your services. What a shame, what a shame, what a shame.'

'Where is he?' said Hal. 'What's happened to him?'

'Not for Mortals to inquire, no, no, not for Mortals. Time will tell, time will tell.'

And with a final caw, the raven soared into the sky and away, until she was a distant speck against the moon. Then she was gone.

Lugh watched it go. 'It'll be back.' he said with certainty. 'Or if not that one, lots of friends and relations. There will always be ravens here on the hill.'

Gilly stared at him. 'How do you know?'

'I can see it,' said Lugh simply.

'How?'

Lugh shrugged. 'I just can. I can see a castle, and lots of people, and ravens.'

'Like the Tower of London,' said Gilly.

'Here, or somewhere else?'

'I don't know,' said Lugh. 'It seems very strange. Perhaps it's your world.'

'Why would you see that?' asked Gilly.

'Because it's very close,' said a voice

Hal and Gilly whirled round. There, standing on the hillside as though he'd grown on it, was the forester from the Wild Forest. They stared at him.

'I've come to show you the way home.'

'Home?' said Gilly. She could feel her heart beating, *thump, thump, thump*.

'Where do we have to go? Is it far?' asked Hal, unable to keep the eagerness out of his voice. Back home! To a place where reality ruled, where what you saw was exactly what was there, no more, no less. No magic!

'Far? Oh, it's never far. Look behind you.'

The hill top had changed again. The trees had all gone, and in their place was the familiar stone entrance leading into shadows.

Gilly took a deep breath. 'That will take us back to where we were?'

The forester nodded.

'Will we ever come back?' asked Hal.

'That, I cannot say,' the forester told them gravely. 'You must take nothing with you from here, though. Otherwise you could be called through against your will. Have you anything? Food? Something belonging to Lugh?'

Hal and Gilly shook their heads and looked at Bram.

'Nothing,' he said.

'Then goodbye, and my good wishes go with you. Face all your challenges as you have this one, and you will have interesting lives. Farewell.'

Hal and Gilly walked slowly towards the stone.

'Cross your fingers,' said Hal. 'Let's just hope it isn't Calcutta in the rush hour in the year two thousand and fifty . . .'

It wasn't. They tumbled out into the same room in the same museum, with the mist just dissolving away in front of their eyes.

Relief flooded through Gilly. 'We made it, Hal,' she said.

'Yes,' said Hal.

'And so, by the sound of it, did Erica,' added Bram.

They could hear Erica's high voice outside in the passageway. 'No, they hid, playing some silly game. It's kind of rude, I guess, and it's very impolite to be unpunctual. After all, if I could be back in the lobby at the right time, they could have made it.'

'That not fair, Erica.' It was Uncle David's voice.

'Maybe, but Helena's mad at them, and I guess their parents aren't too happy.'

The voices faded away. Gilly made a face at Hal. 'I don't think we came through at exactly the moment we left,' she said.

She tiptoed to the door and looked out into the passageway, with Hal and Bram close behind her.

Erica was standing there, with her back to them. She wasn't talking to Uncle David any longer, but to a very tall man with the coldest face Gilly had ever seen. Gilly shuddered, and the man looked straight at her. She felt icy, hostile eyes sweep over her, and cowered back against the wall.

Hal dragged her back into the room with the stones, pale and shaken.

'Did you see him?'

Gilly nodded. 'Yes.'

'Did you see the venomous look he gave us?'

'Yes.'

'You know who he is, don't you?'

'No.'

'He's that man who was with Erica on the boat when we escaped on the canal. The man Jouri said was one of the Twelve.'

'What's he doing here?' Gilly said in a strangled whisper.

'I hate to think.'

Hal sidled to the door and looked out again. Bram

was down the other end of the passage, and he tried to catch his attention. At that moment, Erica turned and saw him. 'There they are,' she cried.

Hal and Gilly dashed out of the door and hurled themselves along the passageway.

'They're going to catch us,' said Gilly.

Erica was running at top speed, and gaining on them with every step. That's what being a champion sprinter does for you, Gilly thought to herself, as she skidded round a corner.

'Faster,' said Hal.

Crash.

They stopped. Erica was sprawled on the ground, her face a contorted mask of rage as she screamed at Bram.

'He tripped her up,' said Hal.

'Good for him,' said Gilly.

'Oh no,' said Hal. The dark man had side-stepped his way round Erica and was coming straight for them.

'Run,' shouted Hal.

They flew down the stairs, pushing past some startled tourists who were coming up the stairs.

'What manners!'

'Those children, hooligans!'

'They shouldn't be allowed into an exhibition like this.'

The man slid past the protesting group, and got to the foot of the stairs just as Hal and Gilly reached the doors to the lobby.

'Mum,' yelled Gilly. 'Mum, it's us.'

Mum didn't look at all happy, and Dad looked furious. Their uncle and aunt had the polite faces of people who weren't noticing bad behaviour but were glad it wasn't their child.

Dad spoke first. 'Pull yourselves together,' he said.

'What do you think you're doing, rushing about like this? Here of all places, you have no idea of how to behave.'

'Dad, there's a man chasing us.'

Dad looked round. 'Where? I don't see anyone.'

There was no tall man to be seen, just the woman at the ticket desk, who was eying them curiously, and Erica, who was walking defiantly towards them.

'Who was that you were talking to?' Hal asked. 'You shouldn't talk to strange men. And why did you chase us?'

Erica gave him a contemptuous look. 'It's nothing to do with you, but I was actually talking with one of the guards. About the fact that you'd gone off without a word.'

'Where are your hounds, Erica?' said Gilly.

Erica looked straight at her. 'Hounds? I don't know what you're talking about. You two sure are acting strange. The sun must have got to you.'

'Sun!'

Erica smiled patronizingly.

'Don't think we'll forget what you did, Erica, or forgive you, because we won't.'

'Time to go,' said Dad, looking at his watch. 'Where's Bram?'

Bram was standing by a large carving of a head which stood to one side of the exit.

'I like this,' he said. 'You feel it's looking right through you. And he looks familiar, somehow. Don't you think it's interesting?'

Gilly and Hal stared at the stone head, decorated with intricate leaf patterns.

'It's him,' Gilly hissed at Hal.

'I know.'

'It winked!'

They turned to Bram. 'Thanks, Bram.'

'What for?'

'Tripping Erica up.'

Bram frowned. 'That man she was talking to . . . He looked like the photo at home of Erica's father. And when he got to the lobby entrance . . . well, he just seemed to vanish.' Bram shook his head. 'Very peculiar.'

Gilly and Hal stared at each other.

'Look at that,' said Mum in an interested voice. 'Is that a raven? I don't think I've ever seen such a big one.'

'It is unusually big,' agreed Dad, stopping to look at the sleek black bird which had hopped out in front of them. He laughed. 'A handsome creature, and look at the way it's got its eye on us. You'd think it was about to say something.'

Hal pulled at his father's hand. 'Come on, Dad,' he said urgently. 'I'll race you down the hill.'

Gilly felt dizzy with relief and happiness as she looked out over the familiar landscape, which lay basking under a blazing August sun. 'Mum,' she said as they walked together down the hill. 'Do you know Erica's father? I mean, does he live with them? Or are her parents divorced?'

'Now why do you ask that? No, they aren't divorced, but I know that Erica's father is away most of the time. Perhaps that's why she's rather, um, difficult. It's hard for a girl not to see her father for weeks and months on end.'

'Where does he go?' Gilly tried to sound casual.

Mum frowned. 'I'm not really very sure. I think he's attached to the United Nations in some diplomatic role. Peace-keeping,' she added vaguely. 'Something like that. Or advising developing countries about their political systems. Ask Aunt Helena if you really want to know. She doesn't like him, I can tell you that much. She was very upset when her sister married him, said he wasn't to be trusted.' Mum realized that she was saying too much and pulled herself up. 'There,' she said with a laugh. 'Gossiping, when I've never met him. I'm sure he's very nice.'

'No way,' said Gilly under her breath.

Hal lay in his hammock, swinging gently from side to side. Gilly sat at her easel, painting.

Erica had flown back to America the week before, much to everyone's relief. Hal and Gilly's father swore he had never in all his life met a more tiresome girl, and even their kind and hospitable mother said she was glad to see her go. Bram had stayed on a few more days until his parents collected him when they got back from Sweden.

'He wasn't so bad, really,' said Gilly.

'Not compared to Erica, no,' said Hal.

Gilly sneezed, and pulled out a large handkerchief from her pocket.

'You must still have some of those apple seeds in your pocket,' said Hal. Then, realizing what he had said, he sat up so suddenly that the hammock twisted over and dumped him on the ground.

Gilly was standing stock-still, a horrified look on her face. Hal crawled towards her, searching the ground.

'Don't move. We must find them all, and burn them!'

'Here's one . . . two . . .'

'Here's another one.'

'How many were there?'

'I don't know.'

'We've got six. That looks about right. Inside, and find the matches.'

They ran indoors.

Outside, the seventh seed lay unseen in the warm, dark earth.